To Louis,

STONE & SKY

PRELUDES

COLLECTION

Onward to
Wonder!

Stone & Sky Preludes Collection. Copyright © 2023 by Z.S. Diamanti

ISBN: 978-1-961580-03-9 (paperback)

ISBN: 978-1-961580-04-6 (hardback)

ISBN: 978-1-961580-05-3 (e-book)

Originally Published as a series of stories in 2022 in the United States.

Sign up for Z.S. Diamanti's Readers List at ZSDiamanti.com

STONE & SKY

PRELUDES
COLLECTION

Z.S. DIAMANTI

GOLDEN
GRIFFIN

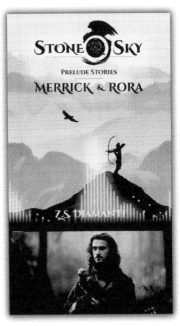

FREE ACCESS TO THE
AUDIO VERSIONS

*For all those who say yes to
adventure and wonder*

CONTENTS

Preface

Often, I have wondered. Do you still wonder? Do you remember that feeling of surprise and admiration at something wholly beautiful and unexpected? How amazing is the gift of wondering.

When I first wrote *Stone & Sky*, I was excited to hop on griffin-back and fly off to a new world. To my surprise, I found myself in a world full of magic, friendship, adventure, and fun. I could not expect where the journey would take me, and even more exciting, how I could share it with others.

Stone & Sky: Preludes Collection is a collection of stories about characters that you meet in *Stone & Sky*. The characters within these pages made their first appearance while I was writing *Stone & Sky*. But when I had finished the first book, I realized that I enjoyed them far too much. I wanted more time with them. Thus, the preludes were born.

These preludes can be read straight through, as so many readers have enjoyed them before. Or you can enjoy them in chronological order as a companion to *Stone & Sky*. At the beginning of each prelude you'll see a note from me. In that note, I give you my recommended reading order so you can see what these characters were up to right before you meet them in *Stone & Sky*.

I am beyond excited to introduce these characters to you. If you're anything like me, perhaps when you're finished reading their stories, they'll seem like old friends to you as well.

As you flip through these pages, open your heart to magic and joy. I hope you can escape for just a little while and walk with me in wonder.

Welcome to Finlestia.

Z.S. Diamanti
July 2023

MAP of TARRINE

A CONTINENT OF FINLESTIA

CHARTOK TUNDRA

ICE LAKE

SEA

TANDAL

STRANDED COAST

SEA

BOROK

DAK-TAHN

RENJAK

RUK

PORAK

LAKJO

EHUN RA

CALROK

ELK RIVER

EANT SEA

CROSSDIN

EALIUM

LORALITH

HILL STOP

ELDERWOOD FOREST

WHITESTONE

WHITESTONE FOREST

PALORI RUINS

DAHRENPORT

EANT SEA NARROWS

EANT

BOLIN RIVER

TELRO

TAMARIA

MARON

BLACKMAR FOREST

PALORI RIVER

LAKERUN

PEARL LAKE

STALFORD

VANDOR

WILDLANDS

LASTTOWN

LAST LAKE

KALIMANDIR

MOON BAY

SEA

NARI DESERT

LIAMPORT

MERRICK & RORA

MERRICK & RORA

PRELUDE ONE

Read before Chapter 1 of Stone & Sky

The wind swept across the prairies and rustled the trees on the edge of the wood where two landscapes collided. Merrick held his falcon, Rora, straight as he swung his legs over a fallen tree. He stayed in the cool shade of the woods as they trekked toward the little creek that they usually followed out into the plains. Bron's Creek flowed into a wetland area out east of Tamaria, the huntsman's home city. Often, however, he felt as though he were more at home out among the wild animals.

Ever since his brother Greggo had died in an encounter with a Plains Bear, the young man had spent more and more time away from the city. He was now the eldest of all the sons of Grell, the master huntsman. And as such, it was his responsibility to help bring in food for their family. He no longer brought his sister on hunts with him, as she had been on the hunt when Greggo died. And his younger brothers were all still training with their father. The last few years had been difficult.

But one day, nearly a year and a half ago, a trader from the island of Vandor came into the market square where Merrick was selling a boar that he'd killed. A crowd had gathered around the trader. Men, women, and children laughed and clapped at something that the huntsman couldn't see. But then he saw the hawk fly into the air, while all the people stared in disbelief.

The majestic bird of prey swooped and flourished above the awestruck crowd. The people could hardly believe that someone could train the raptor to obey such commands. When the hawk flew low over their heads and returned to the trader's outstretched arm, the crowd erupted into applause.

The strange trader was a peculiar elf, the likes of which Merrick had never seen. The peoples of Vandor did not often travel all the way to Tamaria, and it seemed that this particular trader was more a showman than a merchant. Merrick gently pushed his way through the crowd and saw the way that the hawk interacted with the trader, the joy and the bond that the two shared. It was as if something inside him clicked. He had been missing that for so long. Ever since his brother had died, he'd been so very lonely.

The huntsman knew right there and then that he must have one.

It was funny to think back on that time as he knelt next to Bron's Creek and filled his waterskin. He hadn't thought back to the trader in such a long time. When the skin was full, he scooped some of the clear creek water into his hand and held it up to Rora's beak. The falcon flicked her head and lapped the water out of the man's hand. At this point, it was hard to remember a time before he had the speckled falcon.

When the Vandorian trader had announced the end of his show, Merrick forced his way through the crowd to meet the elf.

"Antoril is my name, master falconer is my game."

"Falconer?" Merrick had asked.

"Ah yes, to be in companionship with a wild bird of prey, my dear boy."

"I must learn of this," Merrick pressed.

"Ah, but falconry is not for everyone. It takes real determination. One does not become a falconer overnight."

"Please sir," Merrick begged. "I... I need this."

And to this day, the huntsman could not say why the falconer from Vandor decided to help him get started. He wasn't sure whether the trader saw something in the young huntsman or if he did it out of pure mercy. But the elf replied, "Well, I do have a couple of weeks here in Tamaria. I have plenty of goods to sell while I'm here. I suppose, I could..."

Merrick didn't let the elf finish the sentiment before he unloaded a barrage of questions. He wanted to learn everything he could.

The huntsman crouched down next to the creek as it started to widen into the wetlands. He looked out over the scenery, holding Rora on one hand and using the other to shade his face from the sun. He squinted as he peered out, looking for the right spot to set up for their hunt. A reed blew over and tapped his leg. It was an afternoon much like this one that he'd first met Rora.

He'd spent a few weeks learning from the elf everything that he could about the hawk. Antoril turned out to be an adept and patient teacher. But Merrick's father, Grell, was less than patient. His family needed Merrick to help with the hunting, but every second of the day, the young man sought out the elf falconer.

One day, he and his father had a particularly loud argument about how Merrick was wasting his time learning how to do tricks in the market square.

"Minstrels and jesters don't make good hunters!" Grell had said.

And though Merrick's heart ached, he knew that his father was right. His family needed him.

"What's wrong, dear boy?" Antoril asked when Merrick arrived, looking sullen.

"I've come to say goodbye."

"Goodbye?"

"Yes... My family needs me."

"Your family needs you to be the best version of yourself," the elf encouraged. "And you have a gift, boy. A real gift with the bird. I have never known Shenla to warm up to someone so."

"Well, I'm not a boy," the correction came out harsher than Merrick intended. "I've been caught up in boyish dreams. I'm a man, and my family needs me to be a man. I can no longer play games or be the market jester. I must be the huntsman."

The elf burst into uncontrollable laughter. He laughed so hard that his belly burned and his ribs started to hurt. Merrick hated the elf in that moment. How could the master falconer laugh at his pain? He turned to walk away, but only made it a few steps.

"Wait! Wait," Antoril said, wiping jovial tears out of his eyes. "Merrick, I am sorry. I do not laugh at you. I laugh because, in Vandor, falcons are used for hunting! I am an oddity, even among my own people."

"What?" Merrick asked. He hadn't even considered it. He'd seen hawks in the wild. He'd even seen them attack their prey. But since he'd been working with the elf, he'd never even thought about the possible purposes of falconry, aside from the amazement of onlookers.

"Yes, my dear, bo—" Antoril corrected himself. "Yes, my good man. And I think it is time we find your hunting partner."

As Merrick watched Rora now, soaring through the air, angling herself just right for an attack-dive on a duck, he thought back to the first day they'd met. She had grown so much since then. She was a completely different bird flying over the wetlands now. And he was a different man.

It had taken several days and many talks to convince Grell that Merrick should continue learning falconry. Not to mention, Antoril had to give the demonstration of his life to convince the old grizzled huntsman that hunting with a bird was, indeed, a very viable way to approach their craft.

After seeing the hawk take rabbit after rabbit, and squirrel after squirrel, the old huntsman was almost convinced to get a bird himself. He was old and set in his ways, though. He would leave learning a new way to his son. And though he did not totally understand it, he saw the joy that it brought Merrick to work with the hawk. In the end, he loved his son, and he hoped for nothing more than his son's life to be filled with joy.

Grell, the master huntsman, gave his blessing.

Merrick already knew how to tie a good net, but Antoril showed him how to attach it to flexible poplar poles and bend them to make a trap. The poles would be held down by a little strap and peg, with the net folded over itself. They attached a peg to a long string that they could pull to activate the trap, and the flexible poles would snap the net over the bird. They also built a cage to hold a couple of young hens as bait.

Once they'd completed all the preparations, they set off through the woods out to the east of Tamaria. Birds of prey were often spotted out past the eastern edge, where the forest met the plain, and that seemed like the perfect place to start.

Merrick had never specifically hunted for the birds of prey, but he knew what to look for. He had seen their nests high atop the tallest pines. In his excitement, he stumbled over roots and rocks more than a couple of times, while he kept his eyes toward the tree tops.

Antoril carried Shenla on his arm and chuckled to himself as he followed the young huntsman. The young man had impressed him plenty, and the elf was excited for him, too.

Eventually, they came to the plain and set up the trap. The small hens clucked nervously as they sat in the cage out in the open. Merrick held the string loosely, watching every movement. The long grass and weeds blew lazily in the sunny breeze, occasionally wrapping on the cage and forcing the hens to cluck.

Merrick and Antoril hid themselves in the shade of the trees, hoping not to be spotted.

"I have to keep Shenla hidden. If a bird sees her, they'll fly out of here in a hurry," the elf said. "You watch for a bird. Hopefully, you get the right one the first time."

He winked at Merrick, who laughed nervously. Why was he nervous? He'd caught many creatures. He'd even trapped and killed dangerous animals. But this was different. He noted his teacher as the elf pulled his hat down over his eyes and kicked back for an afternoon nap. The experienced falconer lay against the tree with such ease, and Shenla sat so contentedly with him.

And then the huntsman realized why this felt so different. Merrick wasn't hunting for prey. He was hunting for a companion.

And then he saw her.

The speckled falcon landed high upon a tall pine only a handful of trees away from where Merrick lay hidden. She was a young falcon, possibly only a year old. But she seemed quite interested in the two little hens bobbing away in the cage.

The falcon fluttered to a tree nearer to the cage. As he watched, Merrick was awestruck by the patterns on her feathers. The stark contrast of the blacks and whites, with a hint of greys thrown into the mix, gave her an almost majestic look.

She was beautiful.

And then it dawned on him; this would be his bird. But he'd have to catch her, first.

His heart started pounding inside his chest, forcing his body to heave against the knobbly roots on the ground. Everything seemed to go quiet around him. He no longer heard the breeze through the leaves. He no longer heard the high pitch whistling from the falcon. He no longer heard the cries of the terrified chickens. He heard only his heart pounding inside his chest.

The falcon swooped down on top of the cage, forcing the little hens to flap wildly in distress. The little falcon's talons clawed at the cage, trying to get to the meal inside.

Merrick pulled the string.

The peg slipped out of the leather loop that held the flexible poplar poles together. And before the little falcon even knew what was happening, the net flopped over and caught her. She flapped her wings only a couple of times in confusion, but stopped when she realized that she was stuck.

Merrick looked up in surprise and found that Antoril had been watching him. The seasoned elf had obviously detected the young falcon's presence and had shifted to watch, without the young huntsman noticing. Antoril shooed him to go and retrieve the bird.

She had been so small and so beautiful then. And now, as Merrick sloshed through the wetland waters and retrieved the dead duck, another of her countless victims, he thought her to be just as beautiful. Even though she had become a masterful apex predator.

He loosed her again into the sky to find another duck, and he watched her in admiration as she dipped and floated in acrobatic maneuvers. Antoril had taught him much to care for her and train her over those first few weeks. And early on, the elf even helped to name her.

"Rora," he'd said, as they sat next to a campfire.

"Rora?"

"It means heart," Antoril's smile glinted in the crackling light. "Not like the one that beats in your chest. But the one that's inside of that. The one that brings joy and sorrow. And laughter and pain. The one that pushes us onward to be better."

"Rora," the huntsman agreed as he stroked the front feathers of his beautiful young falcon.

Even when Antoril left to go back to Vandor only a couple of weeks later, Merrick and Rora spent almost every waking minute together. Sometimes even the sleeping minutes. The huntsman took the bird almost everywhere with him. Really, it had only been recently that he'd started to leave her home when he went to the more crowded areas around the buzzing city of Tamaria. Rora didn't particularly love the crowds, and though she was well behaved, Merrick didn't feel the need to force her into those situations if he could help it.

But out here in the wild areas, the two were free. Free and happy. They could breathe out here, and they'd become an almost unstoppable team. And with all the ducks they'd bring home this time, the house of Grell would be the talk of multiple markets in Tamaria. The duo had become quite the prolific hunting force.

But while they went about their work, catching duck after duck, neither of them noticed that a dangerous pair of eyes watched their every move.

The two sat near the low campfire that evening, enjoying some well-earned smoked duck. They had collected two bags full, and there was no need to stay out any longer. They would need to get the ducks back for market the next day. This haul would bring in quite the price from some of the merchants that he knew. He could probably even convince old Gabby to bake his family a duck pie.

The roasted duck satisfied their hunger, but Merrick had also cut long strips of meat from the bird in order to dry it. He propped a long branch high above the fire and let the strips smoke for a long while. When they were done, he promptly packed them away for later, and leaned up against a nearby tree, holding Rora on his gloved hand. He stroked the bird's front feathers as he drifted off. It was a cool summer night, and he was grateful for the productive day.

As Merrick's eyes closed, other eyes remained open, watching the huntsman hungrily.

The huntsman couldn't have been asleep more than two hours when the fire had died down. Rora ruffled and screeched wildly, trying to wake him. Merrick rubbed his groggy eyes and brushed the long, brown locks of hair out of his face.

"Okay, okay," he said through a yawn. "I'm up. What is it girl? What is it?"

Crack!

The cracking of a stick somewhere in the dark woods froze him. He did everything he could to control his breathing, trying to listen for footsteps. The glow of the fire was almost completely gone by now.

Crack!

Rora writhed in his hand, skittering at him.

"Shhh!" Merrick tried to hush the frightened bird.

He put all of his thoughts into his ears, trying to hear anything that would give him a clue about what the falcon sensed. The breeze blew through the leaves, sounding off cascading waves of noise. But the thrum of his pounding heart seemed to get louder and louder, beating on his ear drums.

Crack! Grrrr...

A wolf.

Merrick untied Rora's bell and prepared her for flying with deliberate movements. Then the huntsman slowly pulled his dagger out of its sheath. If the wolf wanted their ducks, the man would give them gladly. But wolves of these woods tended to like to kill their own meals. And that meant the man or the falcon. Merrick would never let the wolf have the bird. But *he* would also not go down quietly.

Merrick stood to his feet, Rora in one hand, dagger in the other. He peered into the dark woods, hoping beyond hope to catch a glimpse of the wolf's eyes in the spotty moonlight through the canopy.

Grrr... it growled again.

Merrick turned to his left, and there it was. The wolf's eyes glinted in the night, looking as some foul beast from another plane of reality. Its gnarled teeth dripped hungrily, as the creature huffed rancid breaths. The wolf was massive. It had grown well, feeding on the deer that frequented these parts. The huntsman would not have been surprised if the beast had taken a man or two as a meal in the past, as well.

The wolf circled slowly, drawing nearer to the man. It growled a vicious rumbling from deep within its breast. Merrick turned to face it straight on. As the monster drew nearer, stepping over the bags of ducks into their camping spot, the smallest hint of warm light gave the creature a soft glow. All of a sudden, Merrick had an idea.

Merrick launched Rora from his hand. For a split second, he was afraid that he might never see her again.

The wolf hesitated, his eyes darting into the air, following the course of the falcon. The huntsman kicked the smoldering embers of his campfire. Embers, coals, and ash flew into the wolf's face. The beast wailed and shook ferociously, trying to get away from the biting coals. Merrick dove to the side and rolled upright, grabbed his bow and quiver, and bolted through the woods.

He did not know which way he was going as he took off, but he needed to put as much distance between him and the wolf as he could. Thankfully, his eyes were already adjusting to the limited light that poked through the thinning tree canopy. He ducked under branches, weaved around trees, and leaped over logs. Merrick didn't slow down for anything. As he ran, the huntsman put away his dagger, secured his quiver, and nocked an arrow.

The wolf pawed at its snout and eyes for only a moment before it sniffed the air and gave chase.

Merrick heard the cracking of low branches and breaking sticks as the wolf barreled through the woods after him. His tired legs screamed as he heaved them along. His lungs were on fire as he sucked in the night air. But he didn't stop running.

Finally, he came bolting out of the north edge of the forest into the open plain under the starry night sky. He ran straight toward a boulder and scampered up on top. It was a decent-sized boulder, but he doubted that it would keep the wolf away from him. His body was spent, however, and this was the only hope he had.

In the distance, he could make out some of the Tamarian watchtower lanterns glimmering like tiny fireflies. But he had no hope of running that far before being overcome by the wolf.

Instead, he turned toward the edge of the forest and waited. He knew that the wolf had been right behind him, but the creature wasn't showing itself. *Smart beast*, Merrick thought. The wolf most certainly had eyes on the man, even if he couldn't see the monster.

And suddenly, high above him, a short distance away, he heard the sound of metal on metal. Then he heard hollers and screeches. And though he was terrified, the confusing sounds dragged at his curiosity. *What is...*

He turned to the north and saw flaming torches floating about in the sky. As they moved against the part of the sky lightened by the moon, Merrick was able to identify them. *The Griffin Guard!*

The sight shocked him, but he was even more stunned when he saw the silhouettes of wyvern riding orcs from Drelek engaging the guardians in battle. He'd never seen the Griffin Guard so close to Tamaria. Let alone a squadron of wyvern riders. The long-necked reptilian creatures flapped their wings with tremendous force and screech with a horrifying tone. *Wyverns...* was all Merrick could think. He'd never actually seen one in person.

Then he noticed that they seemed to be fighting closer and closer to Tamaria. His family was there. What if the Griffin Guard failed to take out the orcs? Would the Drelek warriors raid the city? He watched helplessly as the two groups battled away from him, headed northwest, until finally, he could no longer see them.

All the while, the wolf crept slowly toward the boulder. The huntsman had become distracted by the flying battle. The monster tensed all of its leg muscles, and just as the huntsman turned back, the beast leaped through the air for the kill.

But the wolf received talons to the eyes, as Rora screamed into the creature's face. The monster howled and snipped and jumped and kicked, trying anything it could to get the falcon off of its snout.

Merrick drew his bow back and took aim. The creature jumped about wildly, and if he wasn't careful, the huntsman could accidentally hit the bird. He took a deep breath and released the arrow. The arrow, for its part, was straight, and flew as true as the huntsman's aim.

The wolf let out a quick yelp and dropped to the ground.

It was over.

Merrick slowed his pace as he came to the edge of the city. All seemed quiet in Tamaria, and the afternoon sun shone bright and warm. As he turned down the street toward the house of Grell, the only thing that seemed out of place was him. The huntsman looked as though he'd never been bathed. But with Rora on his arm, two bags filled with ducks, and a massive wolf carried on his shoulders, he looked like the hero of some long lost legend of Tarrine.

Ellaria, his sister, stepped out the front door just as he walked up the steps. The woman's long red hair waved in the breezy street-way, and her emerald eyes shimmered with tears. She stopped and stared when she saw her haggard brother approaching.

"Oh, come on. I don't look that bad," Merrick teased. He sniffed himself. "Okay, maybe I smell that bad."

"Merrick... something terrible has happened."

Then suddenly, he remembered the battle he had seen in the distance the night before. And Ellaria's face told him that she wasn't joking.

"What? What happened?"

"The Griffin Guard was defending Tamaria last night! I've never seen them so close..."

"I saw them as well!" Merrick affirmed. "What happened? Did the orcs get into the city?"

"No," she said. And her lip began to quiver. "There were only a few of them left when the battle was over, but they flew off into the night."

"And the Griffin Guard?"

"Defeated. The whole group of them dead..." Ellaria fidgeted uncomfortably, trying to push back her sorrow.

Merrick set down the dead wolf and the bags of ducks. He transferred Rora to a special post that he'd built for her to the side of the front steps. The huntsman pulled his sister in close and hugged her. She melted into his arms as she cried.

"You helped to gather them, didn't you?"

"Yes..." she answered.

"That is a difficult thing to do."

"Yes... but," she paused. And Merrick pulled her away from himself to see his sister's green eyes. She composed herself, and finished her thought, "One of them survived."

"What? One of the guardians? Where?"

"I didn't know what else to do with him."

Merrick stared hard into her eyes.

"Where is he?" the huntsman asked again.

Then the door swung open and their mother came out. She was a lovely woman, and it was clear where Ellaria had gotten her beauty.

"Ella... He said something," she explained, looking to her son, glad that he was home, but not sure what to say to him.

"What? What did he say?"

"I don't know," the older woman said honestly. "He didn't make any sense."

"I'll check on him. That gash is something horrible. It'll take everything I have to keep him alive. I can't believe he survived this long after taking a throwing axe to the ribs. And who knows how high he fell from."

The two women disappeared back into the house, leaving Merrick standing on the steps with a blank stare.

The huntsman pet Rora softly and gave her a little treat from his bag. "What have we come home to?" He asked the bird.

Merrick took stock of the haul that he'd brought home. It had been a good hunt. Dangerous, but good. He and Rora had managed, just like they'd always done before.

He did not understand what they'd come home to, and after he was done with the ducks and wolf, he'd surely go inside and find out. But as the huntsman lugged the load around the back of the house, he had a strange feeling that even more danger was headed their way.

KAELOR

KAELOR

PRELUDE TWO

Read before Chapter 5 of Stone & Sky

A crack in his neck rattled through Kaelor's spine as he rolled his head deliberately from side to side. The elf did this every morning at the end of his meditation. His chamber window was only just beginning to let light in as the dawn approached. His internal alarm had woken him well before sunrise, like it did every day.

He stood slowly to his feet and stretched his arms out wide, taking a deep breath. His whole chest swelled with his lungs as he took in the cool morning air. He maneuvered his arms high above his head and brought his hands in close. Any onlooker would have thought the graceful movements some kind of dance. But for the elf, it was the way he prepared for each day.

Kaelor loved routine. He loved everything to be neat and orderly. Each piece of his glimmering armor was in its perfect place on the rack or on the table next to it.

Except one...

He reached over toward the table and adjusted one of the gauntlet fingers that rested out of line with the others. It must have settled while he slept. Certainly, he wouldn't have left it that way. Some would think it crazy to adjust such a thing, when the elf planned to put the gauntlet on in only a few minutes, anyway. But Kaelor would argue that order is a prelude to peace.

The elf methodically outfitted himself in his armor. It had been specially crafted for him and his role. He was the king's aide. And while the king had his faults, Kaelor took his responsibilities seriously.

Once he was satisfied that all the pieces of his armor were properly in place, he walked over to the window for a quick glance. He looked out over the city of Tamaria from his high vantage in the castle. The city's famous watchtowers rose above all the other buildings, sporadically placed among the rolling hills that Tamaria had been built upon. The towers were of many different designs. Some elven, some dwarven, and even some designed by men. The watchtowers had been built with careful planning. As the city continued to grow, they built new towers on the outskirts, and never tore down the old ones. In fact, they still manned the inner towers to this day.

In the early morning before the dawn, the towers looked like a bunch of monumental torches. Kaelor knew, of course, that the dawn shift of guards would be replacing the night shift soon, and the fires at the top of each tower would be squelched. But the king's aide always loved that view just before the sun rose. He smiled as he stole one last look.

He nodded to himself, *Right. Time to get to it then.*

Kaelor spun on his heel and left his chamber. He had many things to accomplish today, not the least of which was the king's court. The aide loved the people of Tamaria—and he wanted to serve them well—but he didn't like the days when they opened the king's court. There were legitimate concerns that people brought, of course. But then there were the other ones...

All too often, people would bring unrealistic requests or even outlandish claims before the king. King Hugen—not one to look ungenerous to his people—would look to Kaelor with an air of pleading and ask if there was anything that they could do. The aide would, of course, tell the king that there was nothing they could do for the unrealistic request. At which point, the king would turn back to the Tamarian citizen and apologize with feigned compassion. Kaelor would nod to the guards and they would usher the poor citizen out.

Sometimes, however, someone would come with an outlandish claim that would pique the king's interest. He was always up for a good tale. Kaelor hated when this happened. It always threw a turn in his schedule. *Chaos is not the friend of order,* he'd think to himself. But King Hugen had his own ways.

The enormous king was a man with a particular appetite. Or rather, his appetite never seemed to be satiated. When looking upon the fat slovenly man, people usually had one of two reactions: it's good to be the king or pure revulsion.

Oh, he smiled alright, always trying to be loved by the people. But his glutenous ways were easy to see, and no one seemed to be under any illusion that King Hugen genuinely cared about anyone but himself.

Kaelor had not picked him to be king, nor did any of the people. But the elf had served Hugen's father before him, and King Joran had been a fair and even man. *How had the apple fallen so far from the tree? Was it on a hill? Maybe the top of a mountain?*

Either way, it was Joran who'd appointed Kaelor, and the elf would serve as the king's aide as long as he was invited to hold the position. He was very good at his job, and King Hugen didn't mind that the elf took care of many things that he didn't have to worry about. It was quite the arrangement for the sloth king.

Kaelor sighed as he rounded a corner toward the front doors of the keep. When he swung them open, he was met by a troop of guards standing in straight rows.

Well, except for one...

The elf stopped mid-step and leaned to the left. He stared down the row, not saying a word. A young guard near the rear of the formation locked eyes with the king's aide and fidgeted nervously. Kaelor raised his eyebrows and flicked his gaze to the right a few times. The young guard caught on, cleared his throat, and slid sheepishly to his left.

Now satisfied that the rows were in proper order, Kaelor turned toward the captain of the guard. The human man with long greying hair had been watching and awaiting the elf's arrival.

"Master Kaelor," the captain acknowledged him.

"Captain," the elf nodded back. "The order is given. Change the guard."

"Dawn guard!" the captain called out over the troops. "Tamaria is in need of your service. Man your posts."

Without a word, the gathered guards dispersed. They would each get to their designated watchtowers for their shift just before the sun broke the horizon. They would have a long day on duty. As Kaelor watched them leave, however, he thought that his day would be even longer than theirs.

The captain raised an eyebrow and smiled at the king's aide, "Not looking forward to the king's court today, huh?"

Kaelor drew in a long breath. Truthfully, he was not. But he only replied, "Thank you, captain."

The captain nodded, still seeming quite amused at the elf's obvious disdain for today's schedule, and walked through the front doors of the keep.

Kaelor took one more breath of fresh morning air. He hated the king's court. And for some reason, he had the sneaking suspicion that this day would have no shortage of chaos.

The young guards did their best to sort the people as they came into the king's court. The people with legitimate concerns or business with the king were ushered to the front of the room. The usual suspects for conspiracy and gossip were sorted to the back. Everyone undetermined was placed in the middle. It wasn't an easy job, but Kaelor was thankful that they listened to his guidance and helped to sort them as best they could. Though it would not weed out wild cards, it would certainly help them to stay on track. With any luck, they wouldn't be at this all day.

Order and efficiency, his favorite game.

Kaelor watched happily as the two guards sorted the last few people into place. They were doing fine.

"Uh... sir."

The king's aide turned to address another young guard. He found great amusement in the young man's uncomfortable stance. Guard duty for the king's court was a less-than-desirable station. And unfortunately for them, the youngest guards usually drew the short stick for the assignment.

"Settle, young Travish," the elf encouraged.

"Uh, yes, sir!" he fidgeted and stood straighter.

Kaelor shook his head. He knew this guard by name. He'd had a couple of encounters with him. He was young, but loyal. He always seemed to be trying to go above and beyond. But he was also, gullible. A bad combination in a guard unit. It occurred to Kaelor that one of the other guards may have convinced young Travish that volunteering for king's court duty was a noble thing.

It is certainly a sacrifice, Kaelor thought.

"Come, Travish. The king's court will start soon."

The elf reached out a comforting shoulder tap, but Travis flinched.

"Well, that's just it, sir..." he started.

"What? What is it?"

"Well... how can you have a king's court with no king?"

"What?" A sudden flush of annoyance flooded Kaelor's face. "Where is the king, Travish?"

"Well, that's just it, sir..."

"Travish. Spit it out, son."

"I can't find him... sir."

"Rrrr..." Kaelor growled.

Travish winced.

The king's aide shook his head again and patted the young guard on the shoulder.

"It's okay, Travish," the elf let out a heavy sigh. "You go man your post."

"But I'm the king's chair, sir. The king is my post. I—"

"Travish," Kaelor made his eyes as kind as he could and leveled them with the young guard's. "I will retrieve the king. You make sure the chair is secure for when he gets there. Yes?"

"Yes, sir!"

Travish sauntered into the court and posted up next to the king's chair. He shifted awkwardly. He was the only person at the front of the room, so all eyes were on him. He made no comments. He avoided direct eye contact. He just stared straight, as if he were in formation.

The king's aide let out another deep sigh and headed for the kitchen.

Kaelor's face twitched with concern at Neli's insistence that she hadn't seen the king in the kitchen all morning.

"I had these pastries prepared before sun up this morning," the halfling said, waving her round fingers over a pile of delicious-looking flaky pastries. "But we haven't seen King Hugen at all this morning. Thought he might be sick. Or that you had him on errands."

The elf watched the halfling mill about the kitchen swiftly. She was a great cook. And like any halfling that can cook, she was rounder than she was tall. If King Hugen wasn't a man, Kaelor thought that the round king would have been a very good halfling. He certainly liked the lavish, more comfortable things in life. But alas, he was born a man and easily twice the height of any halfling. That didn't stop the king from enjoying life, though.

"Coming out hot!" Neli yelled, as a human woman weaved around her.

The smell of the freshly baked bread made Kaelor hungry. He was an elf of few needs and got hungry only rarely, but Neli's bread did the trick. The aroma of warm honey bread enveloped the kitchen.

Neli smiled up at the elf's whimsical look. She took pride in her ability to make desirable delicacies. "Here, now." She handed him a piece that she'd just cut away from the loaf. "Careful, now. It's hot!"

Kaelor nodded thankfully, as he chewed with his mouth open, not able to close it around the hot bread. He managed the bite down. "Pardon me. And thank you."

"Now shoo," Neli said. "I can't have you bogging up my kitchen. Go find the king. And take him a pastry!"

Kaelor accepted her commands and grabbed a pastry to take with him. He backed out of the kitchen into the king's banquet hall. It was empty.

Travish hadn't found the king in his chambers, so it didn't seem worthwhile to ascend the king's tower.

But then a thought struck him...

When Kaelor entered the king's trophy hall, sure enough, he found King Hugen standing and admiring one of his newer trophies. "My King," the elf said.

"Oh, Kaelor. Come, come. Look at the craftsmanship of this Whitestone armor. See the way they shape the metal? It's so different from our own."

The aide walked over next to his king and gazed upon the armor. "The Griffin Guard of Whitestone has to design their armor this way. It must be maneuverable and light. Fighting battles on griffin-back through the air is no easy task."

"Yes, yes. But isn't it shiny?"

Kaelor shook his head in disbelief. "Here," he said, offering the king the pastry he carried.

"Oooh! For me? Neli does know me, so well."

He took the pastry in his grubby hands and inhaled it. Crumbs rolled out the sides of his mouth. Berry jelly oozed down his fat chin and onto his robes. It was hard to watch. The king wiped at the jelly and flicked his sticky fingers. A small glob of jelly splatted on the armor before Kaelor could save it. King Hugen decided that flicking the jelly away wouldn't work, and instead, he licked his grimy fingers clean. Or maybe not so clean.

Kaelor wiped the jelly away from the guardian armor reverently. Then, he lifted it back up to the hanger that had been placed specifically for the piece. The armor wasn't all that shiny. In fact, it had taken quite a beating. King Hugen had collected several pieces from the recent battle that Tamaria had witnessed between the Griffin Guard and the wyvern-riding orcs of Drelek. It had been a bloody battle, and the whole of the guardian squadron had been killed before the remaining orcs flew north into the night.

Well, except for one...

One of the guardians had been found by a huntsman's daughter and they were trying to heal him. It had been a few weeks since the horrible battle, though, and it was reported that the guardian had hardly awoken in all that time. But the huntsman's daughter was a skilled healer, and it was generally thought that the guardian would make it.

As the king gobbled the rest of the honey bread that Kaelor hadn't finished, the elf looked over some of the new pieces on the wall. There were a couple of orc weapons. A jagged sword. A throwing axe. A new pike. But the items from the Griffin Guard stung. The armor was pretty beat up and had a deep gash on it. The shield had an enormous dent in it from an orc weapon or the plummet to the ground. Kaelor couldn't know for sure. There was a spear, though a long crack splintered the wood along its length. And finally, there was a long, thin, curved sword. It was the most intact piece, and its beautiful craftsmanship was evident. A symbol that Kaelor didn't recognize marked the blade just above the hilt.

This was a sad monument to the battle. An ever-present reminder of the loss. The battle had been so strange. The Griffin Guard squadron had been defeated. But even stranger was the fact that it had been so near to the city of Tamaria. It was unusual to see an orc wyvern squadron this far south. The thought of it made everyone uneasy.

Kaelor sighed. It could be a long king's court today.

"My King, we need to get to the court. Your people are waiting."

"Ah, yes. Yes..." King Hugen grumbled. "How do I look?"

The elf examined the lard of a man. His grotesque frame, covered in the hideously colored robes, was hard to look at.

"Kingly," Kaelor lied.

"Excellent! Let's go make the people fall in love with me, all over again!"

It had already been a long morning. People with legitimate business dealings for the king were shuffled through rather quickly. But when Grell, the master huntsman—and patriarch of the family that was nursing the lone surviving griffin guardian—stepped before the chair, King Hugen heaved his rotund body forward in anticipation.

"Hello, yer majesty," the grizzly bear of a man started. His blazing red hair and beard were peppered with grey. The huntsman was a mountain. He looked as though he were as heavy as the king, but his weight was distributed into stocky muscle. "I am Grell, master huntsman. It's been me privileged honor to host the guardian from Whitestone as he heals."

The gruff man's words came out forced, like he wasn't entirely comfortable using such formalities. At the mention of the guardian, whispers rippled through the assembly. Much gossip had spread about the guardian's well-being, but only Grell and his family knew the true extant of his injuries and his recovery.

"Yes, yes! Do tell us how our heroic guardian is doing, Master Huntsman!" King Hugen said with as much compassion as he could muster. "We have all been so terribly worried over him."

"Aye," Grell nodded thoughtfully. "I didn't think he was ever going to wake up. But ye know, me daughter Ellaria is a skilled healer. Even better than her mother, she is. But don't go telling Marie I said that, now. Eh?"

People all around laughed at his sheepish retraction.

"Wait," Kaelor cut in. "Are you saying that the guardian has awoken?"

"Aye."

The place burst into excited whispers again.

"Ah, Tamaria rejoice!" King Hugen shouted. "I had no doubts that if the guardian could be healed, the people of our great city would be the ones for the task!"

The tone of some of the people's whispers shifted from excitement to condescension.

King Hugen looked to his aide.

"And what is his status?" Kaelor asked the master huntsman.

"He seems okay. He's been sleeping for a long while now. And Ellaria's been at his side for most of it. He's been well cared for."

"I have no doubt!" the king piped.

"Have you spoken to him yet?" the elf asked.

"Aye."

"Marvelous!" King Hugen shouted.

"Uh... yeah," Grell hesitated. It seemed like the huntsman didn't really know what else to say. So, he grumbled, "Marvelous might be a little too fancy a word for it..."

Someone snickered at the uncomfortable scene, causing many others to chuckle along. Even the king joined into the laughter. Though he did so only to appear as a jovial king before his people.

"And what did the guardian say?" Kaelor asked, getting a little annoyed at the lack of order.

"Ah, yes. Well..." the great huntsman shifted. "Not much, really. We talked o' the ways o' the Griffin Guard. And a little bit on Whitestone. And a little on—"

"Master Grell," the elf paused him, recognizing that it was going to be difficult to get any information out of the man without prompting. "What did the guardian say about the battle?"

"Er. Not much... He had a hard time remembering. I think ye might too if ye fell off a griffin down to the ground."

"Yes. I suppose so," Kaelor mused. "But did he have any idea why the battle came so close to Tamaria?"

All the people seemed to tense. It was rather unusual to have a battle so near their city. If they were honest, most of them were afraid of what the answer might be. But then again, imaginations can run wild when fear is involved. So, the king's aide thought it better to know the reason.

"No..." Grell scratched at his bushy red and grey beard. "Like I said. He doesn't seem to remember much o' the battle. It does seem strange, though, that they were so close," the huntsman voiced everyone else's thoughts.

"I been tellin' ye thar been strangeties happenin' all abouts the western farmlands!" a gravelly voice shouted.

Everyone in the room fell silent, as an older man pushed his way toward the front. He was covered in dirt from head to toe. It was hard to tell what color his hair was because he was completely dusted in brown. He seemed to slink as he walked, and Travish flinched next to Kaelor when he saw the man.

"You know this man?" the elf whispered.

"Yes, sir. It's Mr. Macintroh. He has the farm just to the north of the Rolling River. His wife and my mum were good friends. They—"

"But none o' ye lissened! Ye dinnit!"

Grell shuffled over to make room for the frantic farmer.

"Oh, but I did listen!" King Hugen said with a big wave of his outstretched arms. "I hear all my people. That's why, even as we speak, seed from Telro is being transported for the northwest farmlands."

Approving whispers rolled around the room.

"But ye dinnit do nothin' fer her! They killt her, they did! And ye let 'em!"

The dusty old farmer brandished his walking stick high above his head, swinging wildly as he ran toward the king. Travish was quick, though, and he tackled the old farmer.

Macintroh screamed.

People watched in horror as he yelled incoherently at the king and the guards wrestled him out of the room. His piercing blue eyes, the only thing on him that wasn't brown, let out tears that streaked the dirt into mud on his face.

"Well. Well now..." King Hugen tried to regain control of the room. "Sometimes people just want to complain. I have done nothing but help the farmers. Right?"

The king looked at Kaelor. The grotesque man had very little information on the seed from Telro. The elf was the one that had managed the acquisition.

"Yes, my King. The farmers are being well taken care of."

"Right! See?"

The people in the assembly didn't seem quite so convinced. King Hugen looked around, trying to figure out some way to move this along. His eyes fell upon the master huntsman, still standing toward the front.

"Ah, Grant!"

"Uh... it's Grell, sire," Grell said, a little surprised that the attention was being tossed back on him.

"Yes. Right. I would like to have a meeting with the guardian right away!"

The mention of the guardian distracted the people from the chaos that Macintroh had brought into the room. A member of the famed Griffin Guard of Whitestone was in their city, after all! There would be much to gossip about it around the stalls in the market squares this week.

"Uh... Yes, yer majesty. I'll have Ellaria bring him to ye when he is able."

"Splendid! Splendid!"

With that matter dealt with and excitement filling the room, they moved on to other business.

Kaelor paid no attention to the next few people who came before the king. His mind was elsewhere. He thought of what the dirty farmer had said. *Who had been killed? Why? How?*

There were a lot of questions left unanswered, but the elf planned on being in the meeting with the guardian from Whitestone. He did not know what they would learn from the man, but he wanted any information they could get.

There was a growing unrest around Tamaria. And no one had any answers.

Except maybe one...

Unrest leads to chaos. Kaelor did not like what that might mean for their kingdom.

Not one bit.

SMARLO

SMARLO

PRELUDE THREE

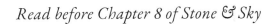

Read before Chapter 8 of Stone & Sky

Smarlo coughed the dust from his lungs. The large tome that he'd just dropped from high atop the ladder had stirred a billowing cloud in the room. The tall, slender orc's muscles tensed and contracted as he heaved. He flicked out one of his long fingers and swirled it through the air.

The dust cloud started writhing awkwardly, slowly forming into a dust tornado. Parchments and scrolls on nearby shelves started to ruffle with the new wind. Smarlo flicked his other hand toward a nearby window, which slammed open. One more twitch of his finger and the dust tornado shot out the open window into the early morning.

"Agh! *Hack!*" someone outside cried, now beginning their own coughing fit.

Oops.

Smarlo ran over to the ground-level window and popped his head out. "I'm so sorry—" the face he saw stopped him in his tracks.

"Smarlo! *Hack!* You try to kill your old master? *Huck!* Have I not been good to you?"

"Master Tan-kro, I'm sorry," he apologized to the old orc. Though, admittedly, he found this all quite humorous.

The old orc mage sputtered a few more hacking coughs before he regained his composure. Smarlo merely watched him helplessly, waiting for the old master's attention to be reset on him. It had been quick, easy magic, and he had not meant to cause any harm. He hoped that the old orc wouldn't be too upset with him.

Master Tan-Kro's eyes fell upon the tall slender orc, still leaning out the window. Smarlo smiled a toothy grin, his lips parting around his small tusks. The old master stared for a minute, but then laughed at how comical the younger orc looked. It was a face he'd seen before, when Smarlo was just an orcling. And even now, it softened the old master's heart.

"You will be the death of me," Tan-Kro said, brushing the dust from his robes.

"You've been telling me that since I was an orcling," Smarlo reminded him.

"Amazing that I've made it this far."

"I have this strange feeling that you'll outlive all of us," Smarlo teased.

"If the king sends you all to your deaths..."

Both orcs shifted uneasily. The old master was known to speak his mind, whether it was considered appropriate or not. To speak in such a way about King Sahr, was considered among the most inappropriate. But his grumbling on this matter was not completely unfounded.

The orc nation of Drelek had been in a strange state lately. Their home city of Calrok sat on the eastern edge of the kingdom, nestled by the Gant Sea. The road to Carlok was rather treacherous through the Drelek Mountains and the Scar Cliffs loomed high to the city's north. In Calrok, they lived out under the sun rather than inside a mountain stead. As a result, they were often insulated from much of Drelek's political issues. But regular pigeons arrived from the capital city of Ruk with news of King Sahr's new zeal for destroying the peoples to the south.

The Scar Cliffs of Calrok were some of the finest training grounds for wyvern riders, and their squadron was easily one of the best in all the kingdom. As such, they had known that it would only be a matter of time before the king called on them to join the new war effort. And he had. Smarlo's best friend, Karnak, Gar of Calrok, was in Ruk at this very moment at the summons of the king. Each orc fort had a Gar that was responsible for leading the orcs, goblins, and trolls that lived there. As Calrok's Gar, that responsibility fell to Karnak.

Smarlo did not want to think of what King Sahr was asking Karnak.

"Where are you off to, anyway?" Smarlo asked, changing the subject.

"I could ask the same of you!"

"I'm not off to anywhere," Smarlo laughed. "I've been here since before the dawn. I was looking for something and then I dropped that heavy tome—"

"You dropped one of my tomes?!" Tan-Kro scrambled over to the window and peered in, past Smarlo. "Which one?"

"The really big one. The one you could use as a cornerstone for a castle. The one you always keep on that top shelf."

"So that no one touches it!"

"Uh... Right. That one."

"The tome of Chartok is not to be trifled with!" the old master scolded Smarlo.

"I know. I wasn't trying to—"

"You didn't read it, did you?"

"No."

"And no one else was reading it."

"No. I've been—"

"Oh, good!" Tan-Kro interrupted again, breathing a huge sigh of relief.

Smarlo also took a breath, just in case the old master needed to say anything else. "What I was trying to tell you is that I've been here all morning by myself. I've been looking for a scroll with knowledge on rankens."

"Rankens?"

"Yes. The miners found me when I went to the Spinefish Tavern last night. They were terribly rattled and suggested that one of their compatriots had a run-in with a ranken down in the mines."

"Rankens... nasty monsters. Not quite giant spiders. Not quite giant salamanders. Slimy, grotesque creatures."

"Yes. So, I was looking for a scroll—"

"Ah well, you're looking in the wrong spot."

"I already poured over many of the creature scrolls, but—"

"No, no. You want to look at the mining scrolls." Master Tan-Kro picked at one of his tusks thoughtfully. "Actually,

I seem to remember a tome from long ago by the old Mine Master Kanjor-Pukra..."

It had always amazed Smarlo that the old master seemed to know where the smallest, most obscure things were mentioned amidst the scrolls, parchments, and tomes of the mage library at Calrok. Certainly, their library paled in comparison to the likes of some of the wisdom towers scattered around Tarrine that had been built by wizards in ages past. Over the centuries, mages from many of Tarrine's other peoples—elves, dwarves, and even men—had been gathering in the wisdom towers to learn the arcane arts and mysteries of the past. *What grand knowledge those places must hold!* Smarlo thought to himself, not for the first time.

Perhaps he had always been a dreamer, but he had a burning passion to learn everything that he could. The mage community of Drelek, however, was a rather small one. Most of them knew of each other, whether through correspondence owls or various visits to each other's home steads. Though Tan-Kro would never admit it, Smarlo had been his favorite student, and had gotten to travel with the old master to several orc mountain steads over the years. When the old master had still done such things, that is.

In recent times, however, Master Tan-Kro had slowed. He did not travel anymore, and that left Smarlo enjoying the world through the largest mage library for miles around. He longed to go somewhere new and experience new mysteries and magics. He got to fly with the Scar Cliffs squadron, of course, but they had only been flying among the mountain valleys to the north or the west recently. He still believed that someday he would cross the Gant Sea and be one of the first orcs to set foot on Kelvur in centuries.

But for now, he would have to live those dreams through the scrolls and tomes of far-gone ages.

"Smarlo," Master Tan-Kro's voice shook him back from his daydream. "For an orc with such tall ears, you sure don't listen very well."

"I heard. Master Miner Kanjor-Pukra. I'll find it."

"Good," Tan-Kro tapped a fist on the ledge of the window. "I'll be off then."

"Oh yeah, where are you off to this morning?"

"Healer Kitia's."

"Are you injured?" Smarlo asked, now concerned.

"No, no. She asked me to help her with something this morning. I'm going to take Taglan with me. The boy seems to have an affinity toward healing magic. And he needs more training, anyway."

"Fair enough," Smarlo replied. A mage's work in Drelek was never done. There was always something strange for a mage to investigate.

Tan-Kro stopped and turned around to face the younger orc mage. "Be careful with that ranken. Nasty creatures... Haven't heard of one crawling out of the dark depths of the Underrock for centuries. Strange times..."

Smarlo nodded in reply as the old mage walked off down the alleyway, mumbling to himself. The library floor was strewn with parchments that had fluttered off of the shelves in the small dust tornado. Smarlo rolled his eyes and started collecting the loose parchments and putting them each in their proper place. When he finished cleaning up, he would find the tome from the old Master Miner Kanjor-Pukra.

And once he did, he would go into the mines and rid them of the wretched ranken.

It didn't take Smarlo long to find the old tome of Mine Master Kanjor-Pukra, *Magic of Mines, Their Monsters, and Minerals.* The old tome was full of interesting things that Smarlo hadn't read about before, and he decided that he would have to come back to it later to explore its contents further. *But that will have to wait.*

The orc mage had only been vaguely familiar with rankens. None had been seen in these parts for as long as any could remember. Most orcs didn't even think of the monsters, but it was common among the miners to tell tall tales of strange things they encountered down below. Rankens were common among their horror tales, and before the other night, they seemed to have fallen more into the way of myth and legend. Though, mages do not idly differentiate myth from reality.

Kanjor-Pukra's account on rankens was surprisingly detailed. Apparently, in his time, the monsters were more prevalent. Rankens were gnarly creatures. They had scales like a lizard, but were slimy like a river salamander. Their lizard-like heads sported a maw large enough to rip even the stoutest orc's arm right off of his body. It could probably choke down half a goblin in one bite. Even worse, it stood tall on eight slimy legs like a spider!

Grotesque... Smarlo shuddered.

The further he read, the less he liked the idea that a ranken was prowling the mines. According to Kanjor-Pukra, the monsters were adept at hiding. Their slimy skin shimmered and changed color to conceal them in the caves. Even with the orc eye's ability to adjust and see well in the dark, the ranken could lurk in the shadows, unseen. The mine master noted that they'd even witnessed a ranken emerge and attack an orc from a side alcove where the monster had been lying in wait for several days.

Rankens were formidable creatures, and it seemed clear to Smarlo now why they were so often the subject of miners' tall tales.

But why now? Why would one show up after all this time?
Smarlo found his answer.

"Rankens are rarely seen outside of the Underrock. They prefer the cool damp crevasses that the Underrock has to offer far below. However, as mining opens up new paths, entire cavern networks are often exposed. This, in turn, gives the creatures more space to spread. They seem to move far from other rankens when it is time to nest. They do so to protect their offspring from other rankens that will sniff them out and eat their young."

"That's it!" Smarlo exclaimed, not caring that he spoke only to himself. "The ranken must have come through a recent opening to find a place to nest..."

He was starting to feel a lot more confident about the situation, even grateful for the old mine master's detailed descriptions. But then Smarlo read Kanjor-Pukra's last thoughts on the monsters:

"If a ranken moves into an active mine, cease all activities! They nest only a few days before their eggs hatch. You must find and destroy the ranken and her nest. There is no way to move them! Once the mother has decided on her territory, she will fight with all ferocity and hunt orc, goblin, or even troll. She must be killed.

But do not forget about the nest. It must also be found. For if the creatures hatch, other fully grown rankens will sniff them out and move into the territory.

Rankens are savage foes.

Tread carefully.

Smarlo had run to the mines as fast as he could. Mine Master Forg greeted him hastily in the chaos of the entrance cavern.

"As you can see, we've sent runners to gather all our miners and bring them up to the entrance cavern," the goblin blinked in frustration. If the mine wasn't operating, then he wasn't making any coin.

"How did you come to figure out that a ranken has entered the mine?"

"I'm not entirely sure it is a ranken..." Forg trailed off as a thin young orc, not much bigger than the goblin, whispered something into his long goblin ear. Forg's face soured, and he shooed the young orc away.

"More unaccounted for?" Smarlo asked.

"You sure you're not part goblin?" Forg accused. "Your ears must be almost as long as mine if you could hear the boy."

Smarlo returned the goblin's grimace. Forg was known for being rough around the edges. And like so many goblins, he was mostly interested in his own prosperity. But neither of those qualities could diminish the fact that he was a clever engineer and had a deep understanding of his craft.

"I can't help you if you don't tell me what's happened," Smarlo said, trying to shift to compassion.

The mine master hesitated, grunted a disapproving sigh, and finally said, "Fine."

"Some of your miners visited me at the Spinefish Tavern last night and told me that they think you have a ranken."

"Those fools!" Forg said, glancing every which way. "Which ones? I heard nothing of this until today!"

"That does not matter right now. I need to know what's going on. Why have you recalled everyone here?"

"One of our new orcs heard screaming down a passageway in the new Gert section of the mine. We opened a new tunnel to a cavern network down there," he noted with a hint of pride.

"Go on," Smarlo prompted.

"At first, he ran to tell his section chief, Kag. And then one of the other orcs mentioned that he hadn't seen two of the others who'd been working in the Gert section. Someone said 'ranken,' and from there it became wildfire. The entire Gert section crew removed themselves, and others heard the commotion along the way. Once they got here and told me, what choice did I have but to recall the rest of the mine?"

"According to what I've read about rankens, that was the best thing you could do," Smarlo gave the goblin a reassuring pat on the shoulder. "How many miners are missing?"

"Four," Kag grunted as he stepped into the conversation. "Four of the best miners this side of Ruk!"

"Oh, calm down, Kag," Forg scolded. "Your team has been less productive than most."

"We've been working the new network!" Kag barked back. Smarlo couldn't tell if the chief's lip quivered more in rage or distress over his crew.

"Listen," the mage cut in. "I want to help you. But I do not know the mines like you. I will need a guide."

"I'll go!" Kag stood rigid as a stone soldier. Forg rolled his wide goblin eyes. "They are my crew; I owe it to their families to help find them."

"Very well," Smarlo agreed.

Kag grabbed two more of his orcs and the three of them stopped into the mine armory to grab a few weapons before rejoining the mage.

"Beware, Mage," Forg said as Smarlo was leaving the entrance cavern. "It's not all mine down there. It's rough terrain. The Gert section is cavern, cave, and crevasse. Lots of ways to die."

Smarlo nodded his understanding and followed the chief and his crew down into the darkness.

Smarlo wasn't sure how long they'd been winding through the tunnels before they came to the entrance of the Gert section of the mine. He'd lived in Calrok his entire life and, unlike the miners and most of the rest of Drelek, he'd lived out under the sun. He felt a strange tension between his orcish nature and his open-sky upbringing while he traversed underneath thousands of tons of rock.

The entryway to the Gert section was well cut, but seemed like a portal between two different worlds. On one side stood the well-traveled and cleanly cut mining tunnels. But when one stepped through to the other side, it opened into sprawling caverns dotted with a million stalactites, pillars, and stalagmites. Smarlo blinked in wonder at the awe-inspiring sight.

Whispering among the nervous orc crew caught his attention. He turned to see a tunnel that was caved in.

"What happened there?" he said in a hushed voice.

"That tunnel led straight down 100 leagues to the Underrock. You don't want such an opening. You never know what might crawl out of there," Kag explained with a shiver.

"Like a ranken..." Smarlo nodded.

"Like a ranken..." Kag looked around nervously. "Come. The tunnels we've been working are this way."

The group weaved through the stalagmites and pillars silently. No one spoke. They hardly breathed. The darkness of this area seemed even darker to Smarlo somehow.

"Arrghhaa!"

A sudden blood-curdling cry echoed off the stone walls. The miners bolted ahead, charging in what seemed like the direction of the howl. Smarlo ran after them, trying to keep track of the turns. The tunnels were a maze of side shoots and alcoves.

"Rrreeegggkkk!"

A horrific screech sounded, bouncing off the walls and through the side tunnels. It seemed as though the monstrous cry came from behind him. Smarlo's mistake was to turn and look back while he was running. He tripped over a well-hidden stalagmite as he ran around a corner, bludgeoning his head on a large stone.

When the ringing in his ears finally stopped, and his eyes refocused the spinning corridor, Smarlo realized that he was all alone.

"Kag!" he whispered through the darkness. "Ohh..."

His head ached, and when he touched his brow, he pulled his hand away to find it covered in blood. The rock had done its damage. It occurred to Smarlo that he might have been unconscious for more than the split second that it had seemed.

He stood to his feet with the help of the wall. Dizziness attempted to lure him back into unconsciousness, but he stood as still as he could to shake it. The orc mage looked to the right and saw several alcoves and a tunnel. To his left were a number of other tunnels with their own offshoots. He knew approximately which direction they'd come, but their pace, the terrifying sounds of the ranken, and the recent bump on his head seemed to wash away all of his navigational confidence.

Smarlo looked at the bloodstain on the large rock and found the tricky stalagmite that had caught him unaware. By doing so, he reasonably guessed at which way he had come and started off in that direction.

It didn't take long for him to become disoriented again, for none of the tunnels were familiar. He peeked around corners and looked down every corridor, but nothing seemed to give him any clue as to which way he should go.

He was lost.

Smarlo sat on the cold stone floor and leaned against a wide pillar to rest. His head was still swimming, even though the bleeding had stopped. He took stock of his situation. The coppery taste of iron assaulted his tongue.

The smell of... the smell of...

Actually, he wasn't sure what that smell was. Smarlo looked around as he started to sniff. The orc mage shuffled along on his knees, groping at the tunnel walls as he went.

Suddenly, he pulled his hand away from the wall in revulsion. Sticky strings of mucus made sucking noises as he pulled away. His nose scrunched. He had found the stench. He had read about the slime of the ranken, but for some reason hadn't recalled Kanjor-Pukra's account mentioning a pungent stink. *How hard did I hit my head...?*

A guttural clicking echoed through the tunnels.

Smarlo slid himself quickly behind a massive stalagmite that reached into the dense cavern air, attempting to reach its stalactite partner to form a pillar. The orc mage strained his eyes, peering through the darkness. He saw nothing. And even his long ears heard nothing.

He waited a long time before he pressed himself up from behind the stalagmite. He regretted it instantly. Now, both of his hands were covered in the mucus. And that's when it dawned on him. Mine Master Kanjor-Pukra had been very clear about the slime that ranken's left behind. If there was this much of the vile mucus here, then the ranken must frequent this tunnel.

Smarlo took several wary steps and turned right, down a side passage. It opened up into a large alcove, and to his great surprise, the orc mage found a nest in which sat seven large eggs.

He carefully inspected the alcove. There were three entrances to the area. The corridor he'd come through and a passage that curved away on either side.

He heard a sudden shuffling from the tunnel on the left.

Smarlo pressed his whole body flat against the wall. The slimy ooze seeped into his robes and dripped slowly down his hair. The stench was almost unbearable. Almost. He could hardly breathe, and frankly, wasn't entirely sure he wanted to. What if the beast heard him?

"There it is!" a young orc voice said.

Smarlo's heart leapt out of his chest.

"Yes! We have to destroy the eggs!"

"H-help..." Smarlo whispered. "I'm over here."

Smarlo tried to pull himself free from the sticky goo that held him close to the wall.

"The mage lives!"

"You destroy the nest," Kag ordered the miner as he went to help Smarlo. "We thought we lost you to the maze."

"I tripped and hit my head. I don't know how long I've been wandering. I can't believe I found you."

"You seem to have found the creature's nest even before we did!" Kag whispered, impressed.

Kag helped Smarlo wipe as much of the mucus away as they could. Behind the crew chief, the younger orc smashed eggs one-by-one with his war hammer. A clang rang out with each swing.

"Where's..."

"Dead. Ranken got him."

"Did you find any of the—"

"All dead. Nothing but bones now."

Kag shook his head, a sadness sweeping over him.

"At least we can destroy the nest."

Another clang from the war hammer reverberated through the tunnels all around them.

"Yes, but the ranken—"

"Screeeegh!"

The ranken mother came skittering into the alcove, her eight gnarly legs clacking and scratching. She went straight for Kag's young miner and lifted him into the air with four of her hideous legs. She screeched again before she ripped him in two, chomping on his upper half in her horrible maw.

Kag jumped into action, screaming at the horrible creature as it reared four of its dangerous legs at the orc in defense. Kag chopped and hacked at her legs with his jagged sword, trying to get in closer to the monster's belly.

Smarlo pulled a pouch of concussive powder from his belt and hurled it, blasting the creature's lizard-like face. The ranken squealed and shook its head wildly. Its legs skittered to the right and then back to the left as it tried to regain its faculties.

"Now!" Smarlo yelled to Kag.

The crew chief buried his jagged sword into the monster's belly. The ranken writhed and twisted, letting out a deafening screech in the enclosed alcove.

"Again!" Smarlo yelled.

"I can't!"

"What? Why—"

Suddenly, the savage beast kicked Kag, sending him flying at the stone wall. He scrambled to his feet and swayed.

"The sword!" he shouted, pointing at the ranken.

The monster kicked and screeched, scratching at its belly in an attempt to dislodge the sword embedded in its gut. When it realized that it could not, the ranken turned its attention toward the orc who had impaled it.

"Run!" Smarlo shouted, grabbing Kag by the shoulder and bolting out of the alcove.

The two ran as fast as they could through the tunnels. Kag seemed to have some idea of where he was going. Though, Smarlo wasn't entirely sure if that was the case or if the crew chief just fled without thinking of direction. They could not see the injured ranken behind them but knew that the creature chased them with all ferocity by the sound of the feverish clacking of its gnarly legs.

Suddenly, Kag took a hard left into an open cavern covered with troll-sized stalagmites, mirroring partner stalactites on the rough ceiling. He hustled around one of the large monuments and hissed hurried instructions to the mage. "Listen, she will eventually outrun us," he stopped to catch his breath. "She will hunt us all the way back to the entry hall. You need to run on without me."

"No," Smarlo rejected the notion immediately. "We will end her here."

"And how do you propose that when we have no weapons to fight her?"

"We will use magic with whatever energy I have left. And those..." Smarlo pointed upward at the myriad of spiky stone javelins that hung from the ceiling. "And maybe even a little luck."

"I've never had much luck..." Kag retorted.

"Maybe I'll bring the luck, but I'll need you to give me a few seconds."

"That, I can do," the mining chief growled.

Everything had gone silent as soon as the ranken had reached the entrance of the full cavern. Neither of the orcs were able to see her, as she'd obviously adjusted her skin to disappear among the hefty stalagmites.

So, the orcs waited for their predator.

Smarlo swirled his arms above his head in silence, concentrating hard on a particularly spiky stalactite. On and on the motion continued until finally, a low *crack!*

A *clink!* of the sword, still embedded in the ranken's belly, sounded off to the orcs' left. Kag looked at Smarlo, who gave him the signal. The mage was ready.

Kag scurried up to the top of a nearby stalagmite and hollered as loud as he could. "Raaaagghhh!"

"Screeeegghh!"

The wretched ranken scraped to the top of another stalagmite. It rambled its way across the tops of the tall stone mounds, headed directly at the crew chief.

Smarlo used every ounce of strength he had left to hurtle the stone javelin from its suspended location near the ceiling in an arc toward the ranken's heart.

The she-beast let out another horrible screech, and the orcs shouted in victory. Her deafening cries bounced and echoed off the walls of the cavern.

But her cries were overtaken by a rumbling as the mountain above them groaned.

The entire cavern began to shake.

"Cave-in!" Kag shouted. "Run!"

The two orcs ran toward the other end of the cavern as stone javelins started shaking loose from the ceiling and hurtling to the stone floor far below. Smarlo dove and crashed into a pillar to avoid being impaled. Kag grabbed the mage and hoisted him to his feet. They continued to run as fast as their exhausted legs would carry them, each step feeling heavy in their urgency, as though they were trying to uproot a stalagmite from its eternal home.

Behind them, the slowed ranken was struck by another rocky spear. The monster writhed and scuttled to the top of another stalagmite. A third spire crashed into the beast's back and she teetered, gripping her perch with shaky legs. The look in her lizard-like eyes was a wicked mix of stun and outrage. The large creature wobbled once more to the side before giving up its chase and giving in to death.

The two orcs dove through a stone portal and into a corridor. They lay there as the mountain finished its rumbling. They struggled to catch their breath, and neither of them had the energy to sit up and survey the damage.

"Hahaha," Kag started laughing wildly.

Smarlo couldn't help but join in.

Kag, catching his breath again, reached a gnarled miner's hand over and patted the mage on the chest. "You alive?"

"I am," Smarlo heaved. "You?"

"Looks like it."

"Maybe you've got some luck after all."

Kag let out a hearty belly laugh, and Smarlo joined him again. They laughed so hard that their ribs hurt and tears streamed down the sides of their faces.

After a long while, they rolled over and crawled to their feet. To Smarlo's great relief, Kag knew where they were. He'd been in the cavern before when they first opened the original entryway to the extended network. It wouldn't take them long to make their way back. He hadn't explored the area thoroughly, but he knew generally where they were.

As they climbed over a ridge up to a path that the miners had started carving out, Kag stopped midway, with a dumbfounded look on his face.

"Would you look at that..."

Smarlo peered over to the crew chief. "What is it?"

"Some kind of writing..."

Smarlo shuffled along the ledge to see what Kag had found. When he finally caught a glimpse, he nearly fell off of the ledge.

"Careful!" Kag grabbed at the mage. "Don't need you falling down when we're almost home!"

"That's dark tongue," Smarlo whispered.

"Dark tongue? Here? What in Finlestia is it doing here?"

"I don't know. I have only seen a couple of the letters. Written in a tome that we're not supposed to read."

"And why's that?" Kag asked, now getting a little nervous.

"I don't know..." Smarlo paused, inspecting the writing on the stone wall. He wanted to remember it as best he could so that he could discuss it with Master Tan-Kro when they got back. "The Underrock is still full of mysteries that we have yet to uncover."

"But, my mage friend," Kag turned to him, concern etching the miner's face like the dark tongue etched the stone. "We aren't in the Underrock here. We close off every direct tunnel we find that leads to the depths of that horrid world."

Smarlo had to admit that finding dark tongue here was a strange matter. He would have to confer with Master Tan-Kro.

They walked through the tunnels, winding their way back to the entrance hall of the mine. Miners greeted them with cheers and congratulations until they realized that they'd left with a group of four, looking for another four, and only came back with two. Their initial exhilaration turned to somber memorial.

Smarlo didn't linger. He walked straight home under the starry night sky. He pulled out some parchment and a quill. He wrote down the dark tongue as best as he could remember. In the morning, he would take it to Master Tan-Kro, but he had this strange feeling that this mystery would not be his to solve any time soon.

Master Tan-Kro may be right, Smarlo pondered. *Strange times, indeed.*

NERA

Nera

Prelude Four

Read before Chapter 10 of Stone & Sky

The sweet smell of honey-baked bread wafted through the small home as the front door flung open.

"Nera!" Devohn shouted. "Mother didn't tell me you were coming for dinner!"

Nera smiled at her little brother, set her spear to the side, and opened her arms wide. Devohn ran across the small living area and launched himself into her embrace.

"Mmmhmm!" she grunted as she squeezed him tightly. "That's because she didn't know. You get too much taller and you'll be able to join the Griffin Guard."

"Really?!"

"No," their mother said, rounding the corner with a fresh loaf of bread she held with a cloth to protect her hands. "Don't go filling his head with wild dreams!"

"But, Mother, I'm almost eleven. And then I'll be tall enough and I can join the Griffin Guard. I'll be one of the best, like Nera. I can be in the Talon Squadron. And I can run all the best, most secret missions. And I'll have my very own griffin. And we'll be best friends! And we'll fly all over Tarrine!"

"You've still got a year and a half," she reminded him. "And if you don't mind your mother, you might not even make it *that* long."

Nera smirked. She'd heard those same empty threats when she was younger. It was funny to hear them now. She hugged Devohn again. She matched her brother's pouting face and shot it over to her mother. Netla, maybe the most patient saint-of-a-woman in all of Tarrine—maybe even all of Finlestia—shook her head at her oldest daughter.

Nera whispered in Devohn's ear, "Go, give her a big hug and tell her how much you love her. It always worked for me."

A sly grin crept across the young boy's face. He ran over and wrapped Netla in the tightest hug that he could muster. "You're the best mother in all Finlestia. You're pretty. And funny. And smart. And you cook really good. And you are the prettiest..." He paused. Did he already say that?

"You're too much like your father for your own good," Netla grumbled.

"Thank you, Mother!" Devohn took the comment as a compliment before he ran off to find his wooden sword.

"You are too, you know. Trying to send me to an early grave," Netla said with a sideways look at her eldest. "You have your head in the clouds. I suppose it only makes sense that you'd go off gallivanting with the Griffin Guard, soaring through the sky."

Nera moseyed over to her mother with a cheeky grin on her face. "I certainly got some of Father's character. But just like him, you taught me how to keep my feet on the ground." Nera blinked innocently as she tried to butter up her mother.

Netla let out a long, heavy sigh. "I wish you would have learned it better," she said, now with a smirk of her own.

Netla set the bread down on the table and hugged her daughter. How had she gotten so tall? She held Nera out at arms-length and inspected her. Her daughter had grown tall and slender, another trait she'd gotten from her father. But unlike her father, Nera had a wild feminine beauty. Her ebony skin shone with a warm glow from the candles, flickering in the early evening. Her large brown eyes seemed so free still. The thick black braid she wore gathered all of her hair and sloped backward over the top of her head like the beautiful mane of a mare. "My wild girl. What a woman you've grown to be."

"I was only gone for a week."

"You don't know what it's like when your baby leaves home. It always feels like forever."

"I'm right here," Nera rolled her eyes, embarrassed at her mother's doting. Then she raised her eyebrows with a wry smile and added, "And hungry."

Netla swatted at her grown daughter. "They don't feed you over at the Grand Corral?"

Though she feigned offense, Netla was glad to feed her daughter. She loved when Nera came home for dinner. It almost felt like she had her daughter back home.

"They feed us plenty. But it's not your cooking."

"Ah, buttering me up. Always had a knack for it, you did."

Nera walked over and grabbed four bowls to bring to the table.

"Where's Ada?" she asked, not having seen her younger sister.

"That girl is quieter than a mouse hiding from a barn cat."

"Reading?"

"Reading. Always reading. She'll be smarter than us all, I'm sure of it. But at least I don't have to worry about her running off and flying through the sky on griffinback!"

"That's true," Nera nodded sideways as she set the last bowl. She tried to catch a peek at the stew her mother was now dishing out.

"Antelope sausage from Bilford," Netla answered the unspoken question. "Best butcher in Whitestone, he is."

"Helps that he fancies you, too."

"What?!" Netla stopped mid-scoop, staring at Nera incredulously. She quickly tried to slough the fact that her daughter had ruffled her feathers. "He does not."

"No, no. You're right," Nera waved her hands in front of herself in feigned surrender. "He gives you meat at a loss for no reason at all, then."

"He does it because he is a kind man and wants to look out for your brother and sister and me since…"

Nera moved around the table and placed her hand on her mother's. She took the bowl and ladle from the older woman and finished dishing out the antelope sausage stew. "He's a good man, you know," Nera said, more gently this time.

"I know."

"And Father has been gone for 10 years."

"I know."

"He would want you to be happy and taken care of."

"You don't remember him as well as I do, if you think that's true," Netla laughed at a memory that Nera couldn't see. "Not that he was cruel. No, quite the opposite. His heart was so big. He loved like a crazy man. It was easy for him. He would give you his heart and ask you if you needed his lungs, too."

Nera chuckled.

"And oh, how he loved you."

Nera looked up from the pot of stew. Her own eyes welled up, mirroring her mother's. It had been 10 years since her father had died on mission with the Griffin Guard. The honor with which the guardians performed the funeral rite for her father shifted her world. Nera grew up so fast after that. All she wanted to do was be a guardian. She had talked to Master Melkis, one of the head trainers of the Griffin Guard, at the funeral rite for her father. Wisely, the old master had made her wait for months to make sure she wasn't making a rash decision in her grief. But Nera was determined, and she used every single day of those months to train and prepare for joining the order.

The Griffin Guard of Whitestone had a sacred duty to protect the peoples of Tarrine from the dreaded orc nation of Drelek. They had been doing so since their inception at the end of the Second Great Black War. Since then, squadrons of griffin guardians would fight off wyvern-riding orc raiding parties from Drelek, protecting all the peoples of the south. It was a difficult duty, but one they performed with great honor.

When her father had given his life in service to the Griffin Guard of Whitestone, she decided that she would carry on his legacy, much to Netla's chagrin. But Nera was like a wild horse running on the rolling plains in the south. None could tame her, not even her mother. At least the Griffin Guard could direct and focus her.

Even though she started her training a couple of years later than most commoners, she was tenacious and attacked her training with an unmatched fervor. She quickly became a favorite among the trainers and was moved into training specifically with Master Melkis. There she had joined a select few students, including some of Whitestone's royal sons. She and Pernden, one of the boys she'd trained with, were selected for the Talon Squadron, the Griffin Guard's elite unit, which received the most difficult and secret missions.

It was funny to think how far she'd come. And yet, here she sat, across the table from her mother, thankful that she could. Netla beamed at her through the tears.

"I know he did," Nera said. "It's funny how much life happens in a span of 10 years."

"I see it all sitting there in that seat in front of me. I'm not blind, you know."

"Hmm, are you sure?" Nera teased. "Seems like you can't see that Bilford is sweet on you."

"Nera Leigh!" Netla feigned anger.

"Should I call Devohn and Ada for dinner?" Nera said, hopping up and sliding away from the false trouble. "Certainly, they're hungry for some of the stew that was only made possible by the wonderful Mr. Bilford."

"Giiiirl!"

Nera chuckled as she hurried toward the back of the small home.

Dinner had been delicious. Somehow, Netla could whip up the most sumptuous of stews with minimal ingredients. Devohn had eaten all of his and then slurped all of the remains from Ada's bowl as well. Nera had told him that he needed to eat heartily to grow big and strong so that he could join the Griffin Guard. That was all the motivation he needed. Ada was annoyed, but had eaten her fill already, anyway.

"I've been reading a tome from the library that Mistress Leantz recommended. It's about the formation of the alliance between Galium, Loralith, and Whitestone to protect the south from Drelek."

"Ah yes," Nera nodded. "It's a well-learned story in the Guard. It's important to know what our history holds. It often holds keys to aid us in our future."

"Mistress Leantz said something similar when she let me borrow the tome *The War Before Wars* by old Master Kendil Berr. That one was about the people that founded the original towns of the north. The ones that were here before they were destroyed in the First Great Black War. Before the orcs and goblins and trolls came down out of the Drelek mountains to raid them. And kill them."

"Ada..." Netla's tone gave the girl fair warning to change topics. "I don't let Nera sit here and talk about killing and battles and such. What makes you think—"

"Oh yes!" Devohn piped. "Nera, can you tell us a story of one of your battles?!"

"Devohn!"

Nera laughed. "Another day, perhaps. It's getting late and I will have to be getting back to the Grand Corral soon."

"Will I get to live at the Grand Corral when I'm in the Griffin Guard, too?"

"Of course!" Nera encouraged. "While you're in your trainee years, you'll live there for sure. Some of the guardians move away from the Corral and have their own homes. But that's usually when they get married and have families. They still have to spend some nights at the Corral, but only when they're getting ready to go out on mission or patrol."

"Will you move away from the Grand Corral when you get married?" Devohn asked.

Nera blushed.

"Yeah," Netla added smugly, rather pleased that her eldest daughter had set her own trap. "When will that marriage happen? Has the handsome Captain Pernden proposed?"

"Mother!" Nera blurted. "He has not. He's my captain."

Netla and Ada both laughed at her discomfort.

"Is there a rule about not marrying your captain?" Ada asked curiously. "I haven't read that in any scroll or—"

"No," Nera stopped her. "But it's... it's..."

"My word..." Netla started, her grin growing by the second. "In all these years, it has been a rare thing indeed that leaves my wild daughter speechless."

They laughed and joked with each other for several more hours. Ada talked Nera's ear off about all she had read since the last time her sister had joined them for an evening. Devohn pulled out his wooden sword and a broom and begged Nera to spar with him. She poked and jabbed at him playfully, letting him get close a few times, only to counter and end him in their fake battle. It was a nice evening. Nicer than they had enjoyed together in a long time.

Eventually, Netla sent Ada and Devohn to bed. Both moaned loud enough to make sure that their mother heard their disappointment clearly. But Netla would have none of it and side eyed them until they gave their hugs and said their "good nights."

"You complained just as much when you were their age," she said to her eldest daughter. "You never wanted to miss anything."

"Well, that's because I didn't know that adults talked about boring stuff after bedtime."

Netla laughed. "Speaking of boring, it is strange to have you home for dinner after only a week. I would have thought the Guard busier of late."

"Why do you say that?"

"Well, you know," the older woman hemmed. "There has been some less-than-savory talk in the market about the new king of late."

"He just lost his father! And who knows what he went through while he was out there all alone. He lost his whole squadron, and then to lose his father on top of it all..."

"No, no. You're right. It would be strange if he wasn't having some difficulties."

"Difficulties?"

"Well, you know..."

"What have you heard, Mother?"

"Oh well, you know Alli."

"Yes, the baker from the castle."

"Yes. She says that the young king hasn't been eating well. And you know what I always say, a hearty heart eats a hearty meal! But it sounds like he isn't eating hardly at all."

"Mother, you can't judge someone's well-being on the hearsay of a castle baker."

"Well, now," Netla put up a finger to emphasize that she might have a winning point to add. "She also said that he hasn't been seen much. Like no one has been seeing him in the courtyards or gardens. No one has been seeing him in the square. And what about the Grand Corral? You all been seeing him out there?"

Nera thought for a moment. In fact, they hadn't seen much of the king recently.

"No. We haven't..." she admitted with a puzzled look.

"Well, see now? Doesn't that seem unwell? You've got to eat, otherwise you'll wither away. And he always was such a scrawny young man."

"Garron was not always scrawny, Mother."

"Well, no scrawnier than your father, I guess."

"And either way, you're turning a lot of gossip into a story. Pernden and High Commander Danner Kane are going to meet with the king tomorrow afternoon."

"Oh, that's good. Maybe they'll have lunch with him..."

Her mother's voice trailed off, sounding distant in Nera's ears as she lost focus on the conversation. Things had been rather strange since Garron had come back from his ordeal. He'd lost all of his squadron. He was the lone survivor of an encounter with a wyvern squadron from Drelek. Even still, it had taken him weeks to finally make it back to Whitestone. Nera had known him since they were kids. She had always been closer to his cousin, Pernden, but she'd trained alongside Garron and his brothers as well with Master Melkis at the Grand Corral.

As she thought about him now, she realized that she hadn't even spent any time with him since his return to Whitestone.

Sweat matted Pernden's long yellow hair to the side of his face. He gritted his teeth as he slid to the side, avoiding a lightning-fast swipe of Nera's spear. He bent over into another ready stance, preparing for an onslaught of his own. His grimace turned to a grin as he lunged forward with his sword straight out ahead of him. The long, thin, curved sword was quick, but Nera had been sparring with Pernden for many years and she knew him well.

She sidestepped, spun, and posted up, sweeping the sword away from her body with the long spear. Pernden, for his part, laughed as he swung back around, slicing and jabbing. She had done exactly what he'd hoped for. She deflected the sword strikes, left, right, down, and right again as she backpedaled, now on the defensive.

A tricky move, she thought, as she found her footing at the end of his combination of strikes.

But now it was her turn.

She twirled her spear in both hands over her head and then around to the other side as she switched her feet, a trick of her own. Pernden glanced at her feet, but immediately back up to her torso, recognizing his mistake. She swung the spear deftly back into her other hand and swiped at the young captain.

The weapons clanged as Pernden parried this way and that, doing everything he could to get out of the path of her wild combination. After several more blows, he did the only thing he could think of and dove into a roll to the right.

Perfect, Nera thought. *He usually likes the right.*

This time, Pernden played right into her hand. She swung her spear out wide over his head, and all in one move, whipped it around, gaining even more momentum. The spear came in low on the second pass and it was all Pernden could do to bring his sword up on his side and halt the long weapon before it struck him. They both paused for a moment, then Nera lifted her spear and tapped him on the top of the head.

Pernden rolled backward and popped up to his feet. Dust from the training ground mixed with the sweat on his face as he smiled at her.

"Alright, then. You win this one."

"Don't I win them all?" Nera teased.

"Come on," Pernden said. "We must have an even split over all our matches."

Nera laughed. She hadn't kept count through the years, but she was pretty sure it was close. "I don't know..."

Pernden rolled his eyes and laughed at her coy remark. As he walked toward her, his stare seemed to cut through her. His hazel eyes determined. The muscles in her body grew warm as Pernden sidled next to her and asked in a low voice, "Care to go another round?"

He stood there, close to her. His jaw clenched but his eyes soft, as if he were holding something back. She fought the overwhelming urge to kiss him. It's not as though she didn't want to—for, she certainly did—but for as long as they'd been together, they'd danced this dance, neither of them breaking. It was almost as if they were testing each other to see who would cave first. As far as either of them could tell, neither wanted to play a game. It wasn't as if anyone would chastise them for it. It wasn't against any rules. But duty and responsibility leave little room for love. At least, that's what they told themselves.

In truth, they were both just scared.

Both lost loved ones, parents, at young ages. Both had been forged and hardened by those losses. But for some reason, the guardians softened each other—a terrifying prospect. To open oneself to the possibility of love is to open oneself to the possibility of heartbreak. It's a road that requires courage.

A strange thought for—arguably—two of the most courageous members of the fabled Whitestone Griffin Guard.

The world all around them seemed to fall away in silence. Pernden inched closer, leaning in, as if in slow motion. Nera's body relaxed as she began to let the walls fall and give in. She did not want to fight it anymore.

Pernden's hand unconsciously slid around her back. She used every ounce of self-control she had left. If this game was over, he would have to kiss her. She would win. But then again, she did not care.

She pressed closer to him and—

"Ah-hem..."

Pernden and Nera were ripped away from the intimate moment. Strangely, their bodies fought against their minds. They had frozen in place, but their faces turned to acknowledge the sound.

A rather tickled Master Melkis stood nearby, trying, but failing, to hide a wide grin. His old face wrinkled in a funny way, betraying his deep amusement. "If you're going to kiss the lady, young Captain, you should remember that we do have a meeting with the king, soon," he said with pop of his eyebrows and a wry smirk.

"Uh... Yes... Right." Pernden straightened awkwardly, wondering how long the old master had been standing there.

"Yes... of course. Your meeting with the king," Nera took a half-step backward.

Melkis let out an amused sigh and shook his head. "High Commander Danner Kane will be down to retrieve you momentarily. I am headed to the castle right now and will see you there."

"Thank you, Master Melkis."

"Thank me?" the old master sounded surprised as he started to walk away. "They should curse me for interrupting..." he mumbled.

"I... So..." Pernden started.

"Later then," Nera said.

"What?"

"We can try again later?"

"What?"

"Give it another go, later. That second round."

"Oh! Yes... Uh... I will find you after my meeting at the castle. We can..." his tone softened and his voice lowered, "try again, then."

"I look forward to it," Nera whispered back.

All of a sudden, Pernden straightened again like he was shaking off some sort of trance that they were falling back into. "I should go find the High Commander."

"Yes... of course."

Pernden gripped Nera's arm with affection and hurried away. Nera's head dipped. *Why didn't you just kiss him?! You should have just kissed him!* She scolded herself and kicked the dirt.

"Hey!"

She looked up from the dirt. Pernden was a good thirty feet away from her, but he'd stopped, turned around, and called out to her. Their eyes met from afar. Pernden scrunched his nose and squinted slightly, looking as though he were trying to hide a grin. And in that moment, neither needed to say a word. She knew, deep inside.

Soon.

Pernden let his wide smile part his lips, nodded to her, and sauntered off with a jovial pip in his step.

Nera's own face alighted with a radiant smile. *That man...* she thought to herself as she walked across the training ground, swinging her spear absently, lost in her thoughts.

Even with all the strange things that they were facing of late, it seemed that at least this one thing was headed in the right direction. And though she would have to muster a different kind of courage to travel this road, she had high hopes for where it might lead.

RALOWYN

RALOWYN

PRELUDE FIVE

Read before Chapter 13 of Stone & Sky

T raining her ears to focus and sift through all the noises of the world around was a difficult task for Ralowyn. It was not merely that her pointed elven ears were designed for superior hearing, but she also had a rather grand gift for empathy; something that had caused her much discomfort while she was a young elf. Even from a young age, she could hear the trees moan when they struggled through growing pains. She could hear the rocks groan underfoot when others stepped on them. She could hear the creek's ache as it slammed into large stones and diverted in winding streams.

It had been a particularly difficult gift to control, but Master Tenlien at the wisdom tower of Loralith, had done his best to teach her. Over time, she had learned to quiet the world, but the ancient elf mage had cautioned her to harness the gift rather than suppress it. When she was a child, she could not understand why anyone would want to have such a gift. It felt as a curse to her. But over her 245 years of life, she had come to develop an appreciation of her empathy.

Especially on her walk.

She had always been a keen learner and hungrily took in most anything that Master Tenlien would teach her. When she was only seven years old, her parents had gone with an envoy to the Nari Desert in the far south and never returned. Little about that event had been explained to her over all these years, but Master Tenlien treated her fairly. Some would argue rather unfairly, and with great favor. Lanryn, another elf around her age who studied with her at the wisdom tower, would often tease that Master Tenlien favored her whenever she'd learn something quicker than him.

She smiled at the memory as she sat on a log in the middle of Elderwood Forest. Her silvery hair floated in the breeze in shiny strands. She took a deep breath in and tried to remember how long exactly it had been since she had last seen Lanryn. In a very real way, she saw him as a brother. They'd spent most of their young life growing and learning at the wisdom tower together. Larnyn was a fine student, but Ralowyn seemed to have a particular proclivity for the more obscure magics. This, of course, was absolutely fascinating to Master Tenlien, and she had received a lot of his attention over the years.

Eventually though, she and Lanryn had reached the traditional time of testing for elf mages at the turn of their second century. Lanryn was given a wand, no longer than his forearm, and sent into the forest for his walk. And in a rather strange turn of events, he had connected to the magic of the wand quickly and returned from his walk only a few months later.

In all that time, Master Tenlien had continued to work with Ralowyn, trying to find the right item for her to wield, but nothing they tried seemed to work. Master Tenlien was so frustrated with the results, or lack thereof, that he even started conversing with Kosoral the blacksmith to help him create a new item. He had run out of ideas. That is, until one night when he was sitting in the third-floor library of the wisdom tower at Loralith.

"Ralowyn!" He'd called.

She could almost hear his voice dancing on the forest breeze as she remembered running down from her own room on the fourth floor. "What? What is it?"

"Come! Come help me."

She hurried over to where she found him, standing on a table that he'd moved near to the fireplace. Gingerly, he grabbed at an ancient artifact that had been the centerpiece above the mantle for a thousand years. It was a long staff, silver in color, etched with intricate scroll-work from a long-ago blacksmith. Ralowyn thought the ancient blacksmith more of an artist as she inspected the staff now, with the limited light allowed through the dense canopy dancing along its length.

She remembered Master Tenlien's look as he stared crazily at the staff, as if he should have thought of the artifact before. When he handed it to her in that moment, the staff hummed to life. Ribbons of light purple energy flowed around the staff, and the magic blazed bright inside the swirled metal at the pinnacle. Master Tenlien stumbled a couple of steps backward, staring at her eyes as they erupted in lavender fire.

"I can't believe it!" He said. "No one has been able to connect to the magic of the Staff of Anvelorian since... since... Anvelorian himself!"

The staff hummed louder and louder in the room that night as it vibrated uncontrollably in her hands. Suddenly, she dropped the ancient staff to the ground with a *clang!*

"I'm sorry," she said, shaking. "I couldn't hold it any longer."

"It's okay, it's okay," the old elf mage answered. His face was the picture of surprise. He could not hide his reaction even while he comforted her. "I will do what I can to help you. But once you can hold it, you will need to go on your walk," a hint of sadness edged Tenlien's words.

"I..." Ralowyn started. Truly, she did not know what to say. Master Tenlien had essentially raised her and taught her everything she knew. It was a strange moment in which they found themselves. All of a sudden, all the normal routine of their lives had changed. Master Tenlien, the source of so many answers to questions she had faced, would not be able to help her with this. He might be able to get her started, but she would have to forge her connection to this power on her own. And both of them had a strange feeling that she would be on her walk for a long time. Hers would not be so easy as Lanryn's.

And they would miss each other.

As a blue-pelted squirrel scurried by her, she wondered now what Master Tenlien would think. She had been out in Elderwood Forest on her walk for 40 years. Of course, that is but a season for the long-lived elves. Still, she had learned much about her connection with the Staff of Anverlorian. Not so much in the understanding of the artifact itself, but rather, she had been able to hone her abilities and tap into its powerful and mysterious magic.

Her eyes glanced over toward the staff that stood upright, suspended on a nearby stone. The purple hue of light that shone at the pinnacle did so in an automatic fashion. She squinted her eyes and the purple light erupted into a mystical blaze. A ball of fire launched from the staff into the fire pit that she'd already prepared. Flames danced to life, gobbling up the kindling.

As she watched the campfire ungulate in a primal flicker, she wondered how long she would be out here in isolation. As Master Tenlien had explained it to her all those years before, an elf mage knew when their walk was done. She wasn't sure she understood what he meant back then. And frankly, she still wasn't sure she understood now. But something scratched at the back of her mind, as if her spirit were trying to prepare her for something.

She could sense it.

She wasn't sure what *it* was, but she knew that something was coming.

She'd only been asleep for a few hours before the Staff of Anvelorian pulsed with magical energy, waking the elf mage from her dreams of star views in distant lands. As she had learned to do some years back, she had set the staff to warn her should anything draw near. Elderwood Forest was full of creatures and monsters that would find the slight elf woman to be a delicious midnight snack.

The *vurve-vurve-vurve* of the staff's magical humming woke her as it was supposed to. Her pointed elf ears twitched, trying to hear what might be coming. Leaves of the canopy scraped together in a loud chorus as the trees danced in the midnight wind.

Crack!

A stick.

Crack!

Another.

Something drew near.

In one fluid motion, Ralowyn grabbed the Staff of Anvelorian and twirled behind a nearby tree. She scanned the forest, peering into the deep darkness. Her keen ears continued to twitch vigilantly.

Crack! Schkk.

When her eyes first landed on the bear, her heart nearly leaped out of her chest. After she regained herself, she stepped out in front of the large bear, which reacted as though she had startled it just as much. "You scared me."

The bear grunted, trying to recover from its own heart attack.

"I thought you a horrible monster."

Another grunt.

"What are you doing wandering about so late? I thought surely a beautiful bear like you would be asleep for the evening."

The bear seemed to pay her no mind as it sniffed the air. The creature's superior nose could smell something that Ralowyn's could not sense. She eyed the bear thoughtfully. "What is it you smell?"

The bear moseyed onward, sniffing the night air.

"Well, you've already woken me. I suppose we'll just have to find out what it is that you smell."

Ralowyn flourished the Staff of Anvelorian, sending swirling lavender ribbons dancing through the air. A moment later, the campfire was gone, and the campsite appeared as if no one had ever been there. She stepped quietly behind the bear, following it at such a distance as not to scare the creature again.

Wind swept through the trees, rustling the leaves of the thick canopy, sounding somewhat like unending waves of the sea. Dancing moonlight poked in through the canopy occasionally, highlighting knobbly tree roots and casting strange shadows in the wood.

In all the years that Ralowyn had been on her walk in Elderwood Forest, she could count only a few times that she'd traveled during the night. It was a dangerous place, and some of the more vicious monsters prowled the ancient forest in the dark. Generally speaking, it was much wiser to travel during the day, even though the sun did little to illuminate some of the thicker parts of the wood through the dense canopy.

Suddenly, the bear stopped and stood still like a statue.

Ralowyn halted her pursuit. She could not smell anything yet, but she thought she could hear something trying to break through the scraping of billions of branches and leaves. She climbed atop a fallen tree that rested at an angle, as though the other tree had tried to catch his fallen comrade. She walked to the highest point, stepping easily over and around branches on the fallen giant. She peered through the darkness but saw nothing.

Then she heard it.

Something was barreling through the woods.

The bear clambered halfway up a nearby tree, petrified by whatever was hurtling through the forest. It was nearly impossible to pinpoint the noise, but something ran through the woods with little regard for stealth. Ralowyn still could not spot whatever it was, but her eyes met the poor bear's as it clung to the nearby tree with a panicked hug.

Shh... My friend. It'll be alright, she sent her thoughts toward the terrified creature.

Crack! Crick! Skut! Crunch!

Ralowyn's elf ears twitched as the noisy intruder grew closer. She could now make out which direction it ran, and she peered through the dim, hoping to catch even a glimpse.

A shadowy figure blasted between a pair of trees in the distance, not running at the hiding pair but by them without even noticing. She could not make out the figure, but it didn't appear to be the shape of any monster of the wood. Rather, it seemed like her. Maybe another elf?

As the intruder ran on through the forest, its pace never slowing, Ralowyn felt the need to follow. It had been a long time since she had spoken with anyone. Travelers did occasionally move through the forest, but she couldn't remember the last time she had run into one.

Perhaps it's this that I've been sensing. Maybe this will be the end of my walk?

She climbed down from her perch atop the leaning tree.

"Rrrr..."

A grunt from the bear stopped her. She turned to see the poor creature, still clinging to the tree for its life. Though it is difficult for most to see, Ralowyn saw clearly the worry in its eyes.

All of a sudden, it struck her how strange all of this was. She remembered elf legends about hags that lived deep in Elderwood Forest, that had the ability to shift their form. They would change their form to entice their prey to draw near to them. Once the helpless traveler realized that it was all a facade, it was too late. The hag would shape shift into a horrible deadly monster and consume them.

Ralowyn had no intention of being eaten tonight.

She looked to the bear again with a mixture of sympathy and determination.

"Maybe we can help each other."

They tracked the intruder for many hours before Ralowyn noticed the footprints getting narrower. She slowed her companion with a mere thought while she inspected the trail. Broken branches on bushes, crunched sticks on the ground, and heavy prints in the moss and muddy areas made it easy for them to track their prey.

The she-bear grunted in the cool morning air nearby. The sun had not completely risen yet, but it soon would. Though the forest would stay cool in the shade of the canopy for many hours to come. A blast of steam came out of the bear's mouth as it breathed heavily. Ralowyn acknowledged her new friend with great thanks. They had not stopped pursuing the figure all night. The bear's lavender eyes flickered as the elf thanked her telepathically.

Ralowyn had only been able to accomplish such a feat a dozen times in the past. When she had been able to connect with the animals before, they'd usually been smaller and of a more delicate nature. Every time had been the same. She had tried to force her way into their minds before, but it did not work. The first time she was able to connect with a creature, it was a deer. Ralowyn had done everything she could to force her way into the deer's mind, but it would not work. Eventually, she let go. She stopped trying to force it. She tuned herself with the magic in the Staff of Anverlorian and it was as if a candle suddenly lit the way. It was not the animal's mind with which she needed to connect. It was the heart.

In that moment, she had asked the deer if it would help her. Not so much with words but her emotions, her heart, her *rora*. It worked. She and the deer played all that afternoon and she was able to convince the deer to travel with her to a far-off natural spring that she knew. It was a marvelous day she would not soon forget.

The bear was not entirely easy to convince, but both of them had been scared. And for some reason, Ralowyn sensed that they both cared for each other's safety. Either way, the creature had reluctantly allowed Ralowyn to make the magical connection, and the two had partnered up for the chase.

Now, here they stood, analyzing everything around them as the trees swayed far quieter than they had late in the night. Ralowyn had easily identified the tracks as soft boots. It was entirely possible that they tracked an elf who had run into some trouble with a monster of the forest. Or perhaps it was an elf on his walk, trying to understand his own magic. Elves tended to be more light-footed than the person they trailed. However, grace is often the first thing to be dropped when fear rears its ugly head. There were a great many possibilities. But she did not dismiss the possibility of a forest hag. Ralowyn would have to be careful to keep her grace about her. One false step in a tussle with a monster of Elderwood Forest could be the difference between survival and certain death.

The pair walked in near silence, each footfall landing perfectly between sticks that would snap under their weight and give away their position. It was deliberate work, especially as she guided the she-bear's great paws.

A couple of hours later, the sun began to peek in through the canopy in haphazard splotches. Ralowyn halted the bear again. The elf mage sensed that the she-bear had smelled something. She did not understand how, she just knew as the creature reacted internally. Ralowyn bent low to the ground, hovering her hand over the tracks. They were very close together now. The runner must have run to exhaustion.

We are close, she thought to herself and her companion. *Be ready.*

She tilted her head to give her pointed ears a better chance at hearing anything that might give them a clue as to the identity of the runner. In the distance, she heard something. She could not tell what it was, but for some reason, her fear melted away and her body felt the flood of compassion.

Her emotions shifted quickly between compassion and confusion. *What is this? Some sort of trick? Are we being tricked by a forest hag?!*

But as they continued forward, she heard more clearly that the runner was letting out broken cries between heavy breaths. The runner had finally stopped, finding some rest in a small section of the forest where the sun illuminated the forest floor through an opening in the canopy.

Ralowyn mentally signaled to the she-bear to wait from a distance while the elf looked for a safe spot from which to investigate. She peered through the trees while she moved and could see a natural well and a nearby cave in the small open area. She could not, however, see the runner.

She hopped onto some low branches of a nearby tree and swung herself higher to get a better view into the open area. And then she saw him.

A human?!

Ralowyn's mind reeled. She had spent all of her life in Loralith, an elven city of ancient tradition. Few other peoples visited. Dwarven traders from Galium would traverse the woodland roads, but human traders were rare at best. Seeing one in the middle of Elderwood Forest was entirely unexpected.

As she watched the man, he continued to cry, hunched over, sitting in the dirt. He rocked slightly in between heaving breaths and sniffs. She could not see his face as his scraggly shoulder-length hair fell forward in sweaty mats. It was then that Ralowyn noticed that the man clutched something close to his body. *What is that?* she wondered, as she leaned on a branch, trying to get a better view.

Her heart began to ache with compassion again. She sensed her connection with the bear waver and shifted her focus. Ralowyn put every ounce of attention she had on maintaining the connection until the she-bear settled back into the bond.

Her heart pounded so hard inside her chest that she could feel it in her ears. *That was close...*

They knew nothing of this man. Was this some sort of trap? And if it wasn't a trap, *What is he doing out here? What happened? Who is he?*

For now, she would watch. There was much about the situation that they did not yet understand. But the elf and the bear would watch and learn what they faced.

She had a great many questions, and she intended to get some answers.

TOBIN

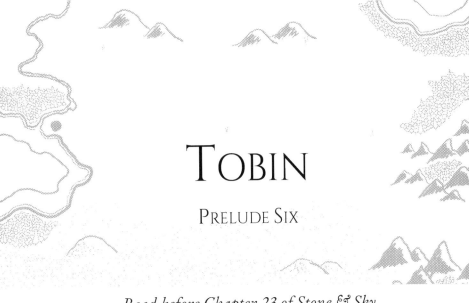

TOBIN

PRELUDE SIX

Read before Chapter 23 of Stone & Sky

The sun was bright in the early morning as Tobin sat on the bench outside his family's cozy home. The hill country outside of Galium always looked beautiful this time of day. The early risers like himself milled about, getting a good start on their chores, whistling happy tunes to themselves.

"Good morning to ye, Tobin!" Ganmen hollered to the halfling.

"And to you, Ganmen! Haha! It's to be a beautiful one, I'm sure!" he yelled back, waving his long pipe at the dwarf, stirring intricate smoke wisps through the air.

Ganmen was a blacksmith with a smithy located in the greater Galium township. He walked by Tobin's home, which was carved into the hillside, every morning on his way to work. The dwarf had always been kind to the halfling, and they smiled and waved to each other every morning when Tobin was in town.

Tobin was a happy halfling. He was plump from good eating and merriment. He was married to the most beautiful dwarf in all of Tarrine; just ask him. He and his wife Lenor had a beautiful little girl named Button. They lived in a wonderful hillside home that boasted views of the Drelek mountains to the north. From his bench in the friendly hillside community, he could even see the great Galium Keep built straight out of the side of a rugged mountain. He always loved the way that the morning sun shimmered and alighted the view before him.

Yes, he was a fortunate halfling.

His hairy feet swung merrily just above the ground as he puffed away at his favorite pipe in between sips of coffee. Lenor had acquired a very nice roast from one of Galium's vendors in the Gerome Market. The birds chirped, matching his jovial mood. The front door swung open and closed behind him.

"I thought ye had to leave early?" Lenor asked him.

"Yes, my love. But I had planned to travel alongside Georl this route. He seems to be running behind. I thought I might enjoy the morning air. Enjoy a pipe, you know."

"Ah yes, enjoy your pipe before you travel on to Crossdin, enjoying it the whole way," Lenor said sarcastically.

Tobin smiled at his beautiful wife. And she was beautiful. A lovely dwarf, by all accounts. Many of the dwarven men of Galium had been interested in her hand, but her heart belonged to a halfling named Tobin. It hadn't been a popular decision, but Lenor was a woman who knew herself and what she wanted. Though Tobin was shorter than most dwarves, save for a few great exceptions that if shaved could pass as a halfling themselves, their love was greater than his stature.

Her brown eyes were light in the morning sun and her brunette hair shone just right. Her hair was done up in a typical dwarven fashion, lacing and weaving, held together by stone beads to resemble a net.

"Button is drooling on herself, sleeping with her hind end straight up in the air. Snores like a plains bear, that one," Lenor chuckled as she stood behind her husband and rubbed at his shoulder.

Tobin smirked, "Takes after her mother, she does. I've always—Ouch! Only joking, my love!"

Lenor pinched him again for good measure, but smiled at her husband, nonetheless.

"Perhaps I'll sleep better while yer away," she teased.

"Can't imagine it. I'd wager it'll be the worst sleep you ever have. Not that I'd wish that on you, my love. But of course, you'll just miss me so terribly. A wagoner's wife must always pine for her husband while he's away. Makes for good balance, I'd wager. Can't have too much of a good thing. I—"

"Like pipe weed or coffee," Lenor said, swiping the mug out of Tobin's hand and taking a nice, long swig. "Ah! That is good," she teased behind the steaming cup.

"Well, that's just rude. I know you must have learned some manners. Your mother always liked to remind me of my own manners. Certainly, she taught you some—"

"Tobin Keeland!" Lenor warned. But her wide grin betrayed the feigned threat.

Tobin's wry smile spread from ear to ear.

"You..." Lenor did her best to bury her grin and leaned over to kiss her husband before he could get himself into more trouble. Though she would not admit it, she enjoyed the game.

Down the dirt roadway, wagon wheels crunched on small rocks and shifting pebbles. Tobin turned his attention down around the neighboring hill.

"That'll be Georl, then," he said with only a hint of sadness. He would prefer to stay and play the day away with his beloved wife. But a wagoner must travel.

Wagoners were necessary, especially in their corner of the world. There was an active wagon route between the great dwarven city of Galium and the port city of Crossdin, which rested on the west coast of Tarrine on the Tandal Sea. They hauled goods and wares regularly between the two cities and made the trip every few days. It was good, honest work.

The halfling hopped down from the bench and turned toward his wife. She stood with one hand on her hip and the other holding the mug of coffee. She was several inches taller than him, and from this vantage, seemed to be looking down at him with displeasure. An uncomfortable smile crept across his face, his teeth clamp down hard on his long pipe, still smoldering.

Lenor grabbed the pipe and pulled it out of her husband's mouth. "Ahem..." She cleared her throat expectantly.

Tobin let out a sheepish chuckle and stepped up on a nearby rock. He brushed the hair from the side of his wife's face and planted a nice, big kiss on her cheek. Lenor returned the kiss with a surprised and unsatisfied look. "Ye can do better than that."

Tobin's eyebrows popped with joy as he leaned in with more passion and laid one on her lips.

"Ah. Much better," she said, returning the halfling's pipe. "Ye better hurry, now. Georl gave ye a late start, and it's a long road."

"We'll make good time. The wagon is light for this stretch. Some wares from the merchants at the Gerome Market and some grains for the millers in Crossdin."

"Well, be careful nonetheless. I always worry when you are out there traveling all alone."

"I won't be alone. Georl will be with me."

That did not inspire confidence. The dwarf had been wagoning for nearly 300 years, but he was getting slower in his old age. And he was old by dwarf standards. Though she did not know his age exactly, she guessed that he had to be near 350. If they ran into any trouble along the road, it was more likely that Tobin would be the protector of the two.

"Ye've packed some meats and the biscuits I made yesterday?" Lenor asked, poking at Tobin's round belly.

He rubbed at the spot she poked as he laughed and replied, "Yes, my love. I always pack heartily. This belly doesn't miss very many meals. And I wouldn't want to start now! I'd wager I've got enough food to last me two weeks if I got in a pinch. You know, a happy stomach lends well to a happy ride. And the journey is as much a part of the experience as the destination. I wouldn't want to—"

Lenor stuck a finger out to stop her husband. "Off with ye, now. Georl will pass ye by and forget the plans ye made together."

Tobin laughed at the thought. "I might be able to walk faster," he mumbled under his breath.

"Tobin Keeland!"

"I'm sorry, my love!" He laughed as he turned and hustled toward the stable where he had already prepared the wagon.

He pet both of his horses' snouts as he did one last check on the reins. They stood tall above him, but he was good to them, and even though the horses seemed mighty by comparison, they respected the halfling a great deal. Tobin climbed up onto the front seat of his wagon and clicked to the horses, who started out onto the road without hesitation. The horses knew the road as well as the halfling at this point, and the trust between them went both ways. It was not uncommon for him to nod off for a short nap along the road. Unless he was transporting a passenger, of course. Then there would be loads to discuss!

"Good morning, Georl!" Lenor waved to the old dwarf from halfway up the hill where the door was cut. "Swift travels to ye!"

Georl let out a garbled grunt, which was his way of saying "thank you."

The old dwarf's single horse wagon effortlessly fell in line with Tobin's. And off the pair went. Tobin turned to send his wife one more kiss, which he blew off the end of his hand, knowing that this was the last moment she would be able to see him as they rounded the bend.

Lenor reached up to catch the invisible kiss and placed it to her cheek. She watched while Georl navigated the road and disappeared around the bend, enjoying the rest of the coffee she'd taken from her halfling husband. It was a beautiful morning, and she planned to go to the market today and talk with some of the other ladies.

But first, she needed to go and wake up her little bear cub.

The day's travel had already been rather long. Tobin had already burned through several packed pipes and a couple pounds of rations. It was always difficult to caravan with Georl. The old dwarf moved slowly, and his single horse wagon moved slower still. While most halflings were quite flippant with their time, they weren't known for their patience. Traveling with the elderly dwarf was a test for Tobin.

They were drawing near the point where the road veered away from the mountains out across the hills toward the northern-most edge of Elderwood Forest. The trip would take them two days to get to Crossdin. That was the difficult part. Tobin could make the trip in a day and a half without the old dwarf, but he felt responsible for him.

Georl's children had grown and moved to different places many years ago. The old dwarf's daughter had moved to Crossdin with her husband. And if Tobin remembered right, his son had moved down south to Tamaria, looking for new opportunities to make a life for himself where people didn't know him. Tobin had never met them, but Georl had told him the stories back when the dwarf was prone to such things. The old dwarf's wife had passed away some years back. Tobin had apprenticed with Georl as a favor to his mother, who had been Georl's wife's best friend.

Though Tobin grew up with his father and mother and had wonderful relationships with them, he saw Georl as a bonus father. One that had taught him so much in years past. Tobin had learned the ways of the wagoner quickly, though, and soon gained an even greater reputation than his teacher. Tobin prided himself on hospitality and giving his passengers what he called a "wonderful journey experience!" The result was returning travelers between Galium and Crossdin asking the depots if the halfling was in town and available. The halfling was quickly able to afford better materials and another horse to upgrade his wagon for a greater yield.

As they moseyed along, his horses deftly navigated a stubborn stone that had never been removed from the well-kept road. Tobin turned over his shoulder and shouted to the old dwarf wagoner, "Splinter Stone on the right, Georl!"

The old dwarf waved him off, but Tobin wasn't entirely convinced that Georl remembered the road so well anymore. Not to mention, the old wagoner's eyes had started to cloud as of late. Even if he didn't remember Splinter Stone—so named for what it had done to so many wagon wheels—he probably couldn't see it in time to shift his wagon safely.

Thankfully, the dwarf's wagon missed Splinter Stone by a hair. Tobin sighed in relief and shook his head. A splintered wheel would have cost them an extra day, and they already had to stop at the wagon camp, something he didn't always have to do.

A couple more hours passed without event as their wagons traversed the road through the hill country west of Galium and north of Elderwood Forest. The sun was beginning to set in the distance. As they crested another hill, Tobin could see the campfires of the wagon camp. He sighed in relief, packing his pipe for what felt like the hundredth time that day.

"Georl, wagon camp ahead!" he yelled back over his shoulder.

Georl waved him off again. He was a stubborn old dwarf.

The final hill rolled easily into the wagon camp. Some dozen wagoners had set up for the evening. They all knew each other, for the wagoners met often and helped one another along the road when one would run into trouble. Though they weren't always on similar schedules, they would often caravan together from the depots in Galium and Crossdin. The wagon depot was where potential travelers and merchant types would find them for transporting people, goods, wares, or any other thing that might need to move from one city to the other.

The wagoners didn't always caravan together, but if their schedules aligned closely enough, it was wise to do so. Bandits were not a huge concern, especially when wagons traveled in a group. But while it was rare, the occasional band of thieves would move into the area and steal from a solo wagon. Tobin wasn't terribly worried about running into bandits himself. He had a rather craftily designed crossbow tucked in the compartment under his seat that he would be happy to introduce to any bandits who thought him an easy target. But he and Lenor worried for old Georl. Recently, Tobin had done what he could to caravan with the dwarf from Galium to Crossdin if possible. It often did not line up coming from Crossdin to Galium though, because Georl would always try to see his daughter before heading back to the great dwarven c ity.

"Tobin! Georl!"

A human woman waved them over as they entered the wagon camp.

"Hanla!" Tobin waved back and steered his horses to an open area near the woman's own. "How is the fire tonight?"

"Already cooking," Hanla replied with a laugh. "I'll throw another leg on the spit."

"Thank you kindly! It's been a long ride today."

Georl grunted a greeting to the woman when he was close enough for his old eyes to recognize her. His horse followed the others and sidled over next to Tobin's, happy for the rest.

Tobin hopped down from his wagon, extended his round belly, stretching his back and then rotating his hips side to side. A nice pop clicked in his spine, and he shuddered involuntarily at the euphoric feeling. After attempting to help Georl down from his own wagon, who stubbornly refused the halfling's aid, the two joined Hanla around her fire. She had already been cooking some fresh antelope meat that she'd acquired while she was in Crossdin.

The halfling's eyes grew wide as his stomach suddenly grew emptier. It looked and smelled delicious.

As the sun had continued its descent, the halfling and the woman enjoyed catching up. It had probably been a couple of weeks since they'd run into each other. They talked of their travels, trying to figure out how they'd missed each other on their routes so long. They talked of the various goods and passengers that they'd transported recently. They talked of Hanla's father, who had been sick for a while but seemed to be on the mend.

Tobin didn't waste a moment. He'd spent all day in near silence, save for the songs he sang to himself and his horses along the road, and the moments when he couldn't stand it any longer and spoke to himself. Between every bite, he edged out more words, just happy to have someone with whom to converse.

Georl ate very little, but enough to fill himself. He grunted a "goodnight" to the other two before he climbed up into the back of his wagon and wrapped himself in an old woolen blanket that his wife had woven for him many years ago. His snores came hard and fast—almost the moment his body thumped down in the back of the wagon.

Tobin shook his head and smiled. He watched the fire dance between him and his friend and wondered how many wagon campfires the old dwarf had seen in all his years.

"It is good for you to caravan with him," Hanla said.

"Lenor worries for him."

"And you don't?"

The halfling shuffled his hairy feet closer to the fire to warm his toes. "I do... he's a stubborn old dwarf."

"If you were rounding 350 years old, wouldn't you be?"

"Ha," Tobin laughed. "I suppose so. But I would likely be a corpse reanimated," he said in his spookiest voice.

"Yes," Hanla chuckled. "Well, you're stubborn now. Hard to imagine how stubborn you'd be then!"

"Me? Stubborn? I have the jolliest of spirits. Have you ever met a human?"

"Yes. But we only have about 80 years or so to be as stubborn as possible if we live to a ripe old age!"

"True enough! That's why you must live well now!"

"Oh, I'm living," she replied, leaning back on her elbows and staring up into the wide night sky. A sea of stars pierced the darkness like a billion paint splatters across one of legendary painter, Jiliana Torver's masterpieces. And yet, even the master painter had fallen short of the grandeur they now witnessed out on the hill country road.

"I suppose we are," Tobin said, uncharacteristically speechless.

Eventually, they tamped out the fire. Hanla excused herself for the evening and Tobin made his own bed in the back of his wagon with a number of furs and pillows with which he traveled.

For a long time that night, he lay with his hands behind his head, watching the stars far above him. Occasionally, he would spot a shooting star and wonder whether or not it was a dragon that had flown too far away from their world and gotten lost among the stars. There hadn't been any dragons in Tamaria in his whole lifetime—and quite a few more lifetimes before that. But it was fun to daydream about such magnificent beasts.

And suddenly a dark winged silhouette of a creature cut through the night sky headed north.

Was that a dragon?!

When Tobin had sat up, shaken his head, and reassessed the situation, he got a much better look at the flying beast and recognized it to be a wyvern of Drelek. While dragons had been extinct for a long time, wyverns were very much alive. The orcs of Drelek had many squadrons of wyvern riders. The creatures looked like smaller dragons, with no front limbs and significantly smoother scales. Their knobbly horns were far less spiky than those of the extinct dragons, and the wyverns couldn't breathe fire. It would be tempting to think that they were not dangerous comparatively, but their horrible teeth and ripping claws on their feet would tell a different tale.

Tobin's mouth went slack as he watched the creature and its rider fly north toward the mountain range in the distance. In all his time on the road between Crossdin and Galium, he had never seen a wyvern rider so far south. He swore that he'd seen some silhouettes of a squadron, way in the distance, flying drills over the mountain range. But he'd never seen them this close to Elderwood Forest.

He did not understand, and as he laid back down in his comfortable nest of a bed, he wondered if he had truly seen the creature. The beast was long gone from view, and his tired eyes could have been playing tricks on him. Maybe it was a big bird. Maybe an eagle doing some night hunting for rabbits or the like. He had been daydreaming of dragons, so it was entirely possible that he had dreamed the whole thing. Who would have believed him, anyway?

The next morning, they were off again. They said their goodbyes to Hanla early after some breakfast around the campfire, Georl giving her his signature "goodbye" grunt. The two wagoners pressed on toward Crossdin, wanting to get to the seaside city well before the sun set.

Tobin led the way again, slowing his horses occasionally to make sure they weren't leaving Georl in their dust. It was another beautiful day and the halfling happily gnawed on the end of his pipe in between bites of another breakfast from a sack that he kept close to the front of the wagon where he could reach it. He wouldn't want to come home too skinny. Lenor would worry over him.

While the traveling was slow, the day's journey proved rather uneventful. They passed several wagoners going the other direction as they went. Tobin waved his pipe with a happy smile and tried to get as much conversation as he could out of each wagoner they passed. Georl issued his most polite "salutations" grunt to each of them.

They had left the edge of the forest far behind them as the road curved away toward the northwest coast. Crossdin was a rather sizable seaside city. There was great fishing in the chilly Tandal Sea. In fact, Crossdin supplied most of the fish for Galium and even the elven city of Loralith in Elderwood Forest. The braver dwarven merchants of Galium would acquire the fish and transport it to the grand elven city via the forest road. It was an ancient forest filled with all kinds of mysteries and monsters. The trip was not for the faint of heart.

Tobin had never been tempted to take the route. He was quite content with his wagoning on the northern road.

Crossdin came into view in the distance, and the halfling stretched his hands behind his back, rotating at the waist until he got a nice pop in his spine. Perhaps he would upgrade his driver's bench with some more cushioning. That thought appealed to his comfortable "experience journey." Certainly, it would not be bad for him to enjoy the journey with his customers.

They rolled easily into town via the wagon route. Houses and barns and stables lined the street that bustled with people doing whatever work was theirs to do. The wagon depot was down near the dockyards, a central place for most of the commerce in Crossdin. Unfortunately, this late in the day, he and Georl would only be able to unload their haul from this leg of the journey. They would wake up early to make their way to the wagon depot to see what new hauls were available, headed back to Galium.

The wagon master waved to them as the pair parked their wagons in the designated area where they would be unloaded. "Tobin. Georl," he acknowledged them. He turned to one of the teenage boys next to him and scolded him. "No. I need you to unload Kenton's wagon next so he can get settled at the stables. He's been here too long already."

The place buzzed with action as humans and some sturdy dwarfs worked around and alongside one another, moving all sorts of wares and goods to their appropriately marked stalls. Crossdin's wagon depot was rather chaotic compared to the depot in Galium, but their system worked.

The wagon master, Dahl, worked closely with the dockmaster to coordinate all transport needs. Fish was the city's greatest export, and moving the vast quantities required a well-organized logistical cooperation between the two masters. Though master Dahl was a rather funny looking dwarf—he was balding on top and had hair patches that stuck straight up and on either side of his head behind his ears—the wagoners showed him great respect in their interactions. If one wanted any wagon work in Crossdin, they had to get it through him.

Finally, Dahl turned back to the weary wagoners. "I'm sorry about that. I trust you had swift travels?" He asked absently, ruffling through some papers that he held in his left hand, looking for something specific.

"Yeah... swift," Tobin lied. "But we ran into Hanla at the wagon camp. That was nice. For some reason, we hadn't run into her for a while. Funny how you can travel the same road, but if your timing isn't quite right, you'll miss each other. She had this great hunk of antelope that she was cooking. Said she got it from a local Crossdin hunter. Might have to have you introduce me. I'd like to get some to bring home. I'd wager Lenor would be able to cook up quite the pie with good meat like that."

"Mhmm..." Dahl replied, not actually hearing a word of it.

Georl sidestepped Tobin and handed Dahl the old wagoner's transport parchment that marked all the things he'd brought to Crossdin.

"Thank you," Dahl nodded, and snapped toward a nearby dwarf who had come to get his next wagon assignment. "A couple of sacks of grain and letters." The wagon master paused and looked up from his papers. A sad glint in his eyes. He mustered a smile and said, "You know, Georl, the way folks have been sending their letters by pigeon and raven these days, not sure how much longer you'll have letters to transport."

The old wagoner smirked, shook his head, patted Tobin on the shoulder, and walked away.

"I'm pretty sure there will always be a need for someone to deliver letters," Tobin piped. "See, as long as there are folks who want to talk to the ones they love, there will be letters. And pigeons aren't the smartest birds. And ravens can't be trained to go everywhere. There are some folks that live out on the plains. How would they get their letters without messengers? I remember a long time ago when I was just a quarterling, my father once told me—"

"Do you have your transport parchment, Tobin?" Dahl interrupted, handing Georl's to the waiting dwarf, who instantly headed for the wagon to begin unloading.

"Ah, yes. Here," Tobin handed it over. "I always keep it in this pouch for safekeeping. You never know when you'll run into weather on the road. And then, of course, there's been times where it rained so hard that it soaked me through my cloak and all the way into my bones. Never been colder than that. That was before I got a thicker cloak for such occasions. But got the pouch too because I didn't want to have another situation with a destroyed transport parchment. That's never a —"

Dahl held up a thick dwarven finger in front of the halfling, halting him mid-sentence. He hadn't heard anything that Tobin had said, but instead scanned the parchment, finding everything to be in order. "Trenth," he called to one of the teenage humans. "Go ahead and unload Tobin's wagon, please."

"Yes, sir," the young man said, taking the parchment and hustling toward Tobin's cart.

"Any chance you have any unassigned travelers needing a ride to Galium for tomorrow?" Tobin asked with more hope in his voice than he intended to show.

"No. Three requested. Three assigned."

The halfling clicked his teeth and scratched at his wild, curly hair. He couldn't help but think that he might have been able to get some travelers if they had arrived sooner.

"Alright. Well, if any come up, I'll be trying to head back to Galium tomorrow. I'd rather not stay two nights at the inn.

Lenor promised that she would make lamb stew if I hurried home. I'd wager there's not a halfling or dwarf in the world that would want to miss that date, you know. I'm thinking it might be—"

"We'll do haul posts in the morning like we always do," Dahl said, interrupting what he expected to be the start of another long conversation with the halfling. The dwarf liked Tobin just fine, and he found him to be a quite capable wagoner with a reputation for taking good care of travelers. But the job of wagon master did not lend itself to elongated conversations. Suddenly his eyes brightened as another wagon came rolling down the road in the distance, giving him his out. "Ah, well. Excuse me Tobin. I must finish this before the next wagon gets here. Good night."

Dahl walked off, sorting through his parchments as loading folks came running back to him after completing their tasks.

Tobin joined Georl back at their wagons, which had been unloaded in impressive time. As they moved their wagons toward the stables, the halfling smiled and gnawed on his pipe as he spoke to the old wagoner out of the side of his mouth. "You think Dahl ever takes time away from the depot? His wife must not be very happy with him. Then again, I've never known him to be a very good conversationalist. Perhaps she prefers it this way. I'm thinking that..."

At a certain point, Tobin spoke more to himself than the old wagoner. It was strange how quickly Georl could get his solo wagon to move when he was ready to turn in for the evening. He would certainly race off—as fast as an old dwarf can shuffle his short legs—to see his daughter and his grandchildren. Tobin guessed that Georl would want to stay in Crossdin for at least two nights. He always did. But the halfling would gladly take whatever hauls he could get tomorrow and be on his way home.

The next day, Tobin joined another halfling wagoner as the first ones to the depot. It was important for them to arrive early enough to get near the front where Dahl, the wagon master, would be calling out the haul posts. Being a bit shorter than dwarves, they needed to be where the wagon master would see them when they wanted to claim and take on a haul.

Human and dwarven wagoners also came into the depot as everyone began to gather for the posts. It always felt to Tobin that Dahl used his authority to make everyone wait and recognize his importance. The halfling didn't blame him, of course. The wagon master was constantly running around, trying to coordinate many different tasks all at the same time. It was probably the best part of his day. A quiet moment before the mayhem.

As the haul posts were announced, wagoners from all over the room would yell out, "Here!" to signal that they wanted a particular haul. Dahl merely called them out and handed each transport parchment to one of the depot workers, who would run it to the wagoner. "Here" was the only thing one could say to get a haul. If a wagoner tried to say anything more than that, another would call "Here" and the original would be passed over. It was a particularly difficult game for Tobin, but he'd learned the rules over time and figured out how to get his hauls.

He had also created for himself quite the reputation with passengers, which afforded him other opportunities when someone needed transport last minute. He always left a little after midday from Crossdin just in case he could get a late passenger. It did not ruin his plans. Without Georl, the halfling could make the trip quicker and had no problems wagoning through the night. And anyway, passengers were worth it. Not only did they bring more coin than hauls, they also offered the halfling new conversations to be had! And he could hardly put a price on that.

Tobin had hoped that Dahl would call out a new passenger request. But when the dwarven wagon master was getting down to his last few parchments, the halfling took one that sounded good enough.

He left the depot and went back to the inn to enjoy another breakfast and had a wonderful conversation with a local human who just so happened to be a huntsman. Not the same one who'd sold the antelope to Hanla, but apparently he'd seen plenty of the animals recently.

Tobin took his time to walk around Crossdin, knowing that many of the other wagons had been in a hurry to get their hauls and get on the road. But the halfling walked around the city, taking in the sights. When he went back to the depot, it would be less busy. Not quiet by any means. But less busy.

He walked down to the docks and skipped rocks with a couple of kids who marveled at his great talent for it.

"It's all in the wrist, you see. If you fling it just right, I'd wager you could hit that ship just outside the harbor! I once knew a dwarf—strongest I ever met—and I bet he could skip one of you right across this water," he teased.

"Wow! Could he skip you too?!"

"Ha! No way," Tobin replied. "I'm much too round!"

They all laughed and chatted for a long while. It made the halfling miss his little Button. He moseyed along until it was time for lunch and headed back to the inn. This time, he filled his belly to bursting with bread, a berry jam, and a delicious hunk of local cheese prepared by a dairy farmer who lived just southeast of the city. Tobin asked the barmaid to give his compliments to the farmer as the halfling prepared to leave the inn.

Suddenly, a couple of fishermen came strolling into the place, talking boisterously over one another.

"Right out of the sea!"

"I can't believe it."

"Where do you think they come from?"

"Who knows! Better question is how?!"

"You say that they sold their boat?"

"Yeah! Saw Lonnie and Kelt rowing it away."

"Where are they headed?"

"Who knows..."

Tobin had heard all that he needed to hear. Perhaps these new strangers were in need of transport to Galium. And he just so happened to know the perfect wagoner to take them there.

The halfling hustled back to the wagon depot and found Dahl, shuffling through parchments and handing out instructions to his workers, who buzzed around.

"Ah, Tobin. You're ready to load?"

"Yes, I'm getting ready to leave. I heard—"

"Well, find Trenth when your wagon is parked. He'll load up your haul."

"Right. I'll do that, of course. But I heard that there may be some passengers that need transport to Galium."

Dahl stopped. He looked away from his parchments and his eyes landed on the round halfling in front of him. "And where did you hear that?"

"Uh, well... you see. I was at the inn having a wonderful lunch. Had a wonderful loaf of grain bread and some sort of berry jam. The flavors were *muah!*" the halfling kissed his fingertips and opened his hand in a magical flourish. "And the cheese... Did you know that you have some amazing cheese farmers here in Crossdin? Honestly, I was so surprised that I told—"

"You know what?" Dahl said, raising his hands in surrender. "It doesn't matter."

"So, I can have them?"

"The strangers already talked to the dockmaster, and he gave them your name."

"Wonderful! You're too kind, Dahl. I don't care what your wife thinks of you. Well, then again, I don't know your wife. But I've been thinking that since you spend all your time here at the depot, she'd either be less-than-pleased with you or she'd be rather pleased about the circumstances because you are not the best conversationalist I've ever met. But I like you just fine."

"Mhmm," Dahl nodded, looking at his parchments again, having heard nothing the halfling was saying.

Tobin practically skipped to the stables to prep his wagon and horses. He only made it about halfway before he got a little stomach cramp. But he hurried along nonetheless.

The halfling did not know anything about the strangers, nor did he care. He only knew that he loved being a wagoner, especially on trips when he had passengers.

LOTMEAG

LOTMEAG

PRELUDE SEVEN

Read before Chapter 26 of Stone & Sky

Lotmeag Kandersaw strode through the stone hallways at a determined pace. He was the very picture of a dwarven warrior. He was a barrel of a dwarf and his heavy armor made him look even stouter. His brown hair flowed out the back of his helm, which had a singular horn on top with long, dyed red hairs that spat out the point. His beard hung out over his chest plate with impressive thickness. He had a rather serious way about him, for a young dwarf, that inspired other dwarven warriors. That was probably a contributing factor as to why Bendur Clagstack, leader of the garvawk warriors of Galium, chose to elevate Lotmeag as his second-in-command.

In truth, Bendur Clagstack was an old garvawk warrior, and though he would never even entertain talk of him retiring, they both knew that he needed to train up a successor because he wouldn't be around forever. A dwarf could live to a good ripe age of 350 years old. But that was not the case for garvwak warriors. The strain of connecting with the panther-like flying creatures had an effect on their dwarven bodies—and that was aside from the very real fact that the older they got, the more vulnerable they were in battle. No, the garvawk warrior's life was not a long-lived one, but many dwarven warriors vied for the honor to serve with the group and the exotic beasts.

Garvawks were beautiful and deadly creatures. They resembled the blackest of panthers and sported elegant, bat-like wings. If inspected closely, one could find variations in their coats that revealed wild spots or markings. But getting that close to a garvawk in the wild would almost certainly mean death. So usually, only the warriors that worked directly with the great cats witnessed such things. They were not very common creatures, and it was quite the endeavor to procure another for the group. That's why it was so exciting to be on a *glendon* team—an ancient dwarven word that roughly translated to "the hunt."

It had been reported that a garvawk was spotted in a newer cavern that had been opened in Galium's famed Deep Mines. Garvawk behaviors varied widely. Some had been known to act like bats that left their caves at night to find prey and eat under the open night sky. Some had been known to prowl around in far-flung caverns, tearing apart creatures that dared to venture into their territory. Lotmeag guessed there was probably a much larger number of garvawks living among the monsters in the depths of the Underrock that the dwarves knew little about. It was unwise to mine anywhere near the Underrock and generations of dwarves avoided the dark mysteries there.

But this garvawk sighting seemed to be a rather clear case. The miners had broken through to another cavern that actually opened upward. It led down several paths and to various side caverns, but also to an opening on the edge of a mountain valley. This garvawk seemed to be one that liked to leave its cave and hunt creatures at night. It was as good a prospect for the warriors as they'd had in years.

One of Galium's war-hog warriors had been chosen to be on the *glendon* team, as was their tradition. His name was Felton, and he had proven himself a sturdy dwarf. He was a great candidate for the garvawk warriors and he had earned the honor. The other half was willingness. No one was forced to be a garvawk warrior. It came with consequences, they knew. So, each one had volunteered to serve with the elite group. Felton was no different.

When the report about the garvawk had come, Bendur Clagstack had charged Lotmeag to lead the *glendon* team. He'd been a part of several over the years, after his own initial hunt when he first connected with his garvawk, Glory. But this was the first one he would lead. Thankfully, he would have the aid of an experienced mage, Argus Azulekor.

As he turned down another hallway, he heard an explosion and bright lights flashed underneath the doorway at the end of the corridor. Lotmeag jumped into a sprint. He started banging on the door. "Argus! Are ye all right in there?!"

"Oops..." Lotmeag heard a weak voice through the door, followed by some rather violent coughing.

A strange odor started burning the garvawk warrior's nostrils. It was an earthy smell mixed with a chalky bitter scent that he did not recognize. "Argus?" He called again.

The coughing grew closer and the metal door loop clunked and shifted as the heavy door swung open. A yellowish cloud poured out into the hallway. "What are ye doing in here? *Huck!*" Lotmeag asked as the smoke clogged his airway as well. He hurried past the older dwarf and opened one of the windows, grabbing a leather parchment cover and wafting the smoke out into the open air. Thankfully, the mage had an anterior room in the castle that had windows.

Argus turned back over his shoulder and smiled sheepishly at the garvawk warrior while he used a cloak to waft smoke out of the other window that he'd just opened. "Not... *Hack!* Exactly what I was going for."

"I imagine not," Lotmeag replied, waving the wide piece of leather. "What were ye trying to do?"

"I've been attempting to complete the work of the old Master Mage Lontus Glonet. He was trying to mix two metals that he thought would make some strong armor that was even easier to imbue with magical properties. *Cough!* But they don't seem to like each other. So, I was trying to break them down even more, and well..." He paused and held his hands up in the air. "You see, the results."

Lotmeag shook his head and set the parchment cover on the table next to him. The air in the room was already clearing and the cross breeze between the two open windows would freshen it the rest of the way. "Maybe open the windows next time."

"I think that's wise counsel, mighty Lotmeag!" Argus laughed.

The old mage was not from Galium, originally. He had lived in the great dwarven city of Kalimandir in the far south of Tarrine before coming to Galium. Lotmeag found him to be rather odd sometimes, but the mage had been kind to him in most of their interactions and he was often willing to explain things in more detail if the warrior was curious about something.

"Are ye all right?" Lotmeag asked as he watched the old mage lean on a table covered in scrolls and glass containers, catching his breath.

"Oh fine. Just fine," the mage waved him off the subject. "And you? Are you all right?"

"Yes. It's an exciting day," Lotmeag's eyebrows popped, and a smirk grew across his face, barely visible under thick beard.

"Why's that?" Argus asked, hungrily. Though Lotmeag was seen as a serious dwarf, for some reason, teasing the old mage's curiosity brought out a fun, light-hearted side of the warrior. The mage's eyes grew wide in anticipation as he leaned forward, turning his head slightly as if his ears were waiting to catch some intriguing news.

"I'm gathering a *glendon* team."

Lotmeag's smiled grew even wider. And after a moment, Argus's chin raised and his expression shifted as realization dawned on him.

"You're leading the team," he said approvingly.

"Aye. Felton was chosen, and he accepted the honor."

"A good choice. He will make a fine garvawk warrior."

"Aye, agreed. They are preparing for departure. Are ye ready to go?"

"I don't know..." the mage said slowly, as his face scrunched.

Lotmeag's heart dropped. They needed the mage. Every *glendon* team needed a mage. They wouldn't be successful without one. This was Lotmeag's first team completely under his leadership, and he may have gathered everyone too early, not having his mage lined up. He wondered how they'd all look at him if he had to tell them that they needed to postpone.

A wry grin crept across Argus's visage, crinkling the crow's feet at the corners of his eyes.

"Ye're teasing me..."

"Only because you tease me," the old mage chuckled. "Let me clean this up. It's a dangerous combination... clearly."

The *glendon* team consisted of Argus, Felton, Lotmeag, and two other garvawk warriors, Dorbin and Kel. The teams were usually this size, as it gave them the ability to capture the garvawk, but they weren't so many as to give away their positions or cause them to be tripping all over each other in the heat of the capture.

They were taking a break at a mountain creek to water their war-hogs and enjoy some shade underneath the pines. It was funny to Lotmeag how it always felt like such a slow process while riding war-hogs. Obviously, he had gotten quite used to the garvawks flying speed—and maybe he was a little spoiled.

The war-hogs of Galium were well-trained beasts that stood just as high, and higher in some cases, than their dwarven riders. The war-hog cavalry husbanded the creatures and trained them for battle. Many an unlucky goblin had died by a vicious gouging tusk of a Galium war-hog. They were heavy, formidable beasts that had sturdy constitutions and surprising quickness on the battlefield. Of course, their speed was determined by the terrain that they traversed, which gave garvawks a distinct advantage.

Nonetheless, the *glendon* team was making good progress. Lotmeag patted the war-hog that was loaned to him for the trip. Its name was Grub. He thought it a funny name, but the cavalry dwarf had explained to him that when the war-hog was born, it had looked like a giant grub. A disgusting picture in Lotmeag's mind. But Grub was of good temperament and rode easily for the garvawk warrior. He was glad for it.

They couldn't fly on garvawk back because each garvawk was connected to a dwarven warrior. It was a difficult process, and attempting to change a garvawk's connection was cumbersome, and in some instances, dangerous. That meant that, while Lotmeag, Dorbin, and Kel would be able to ride, Argus and Felton wouldn't. War-hog was the traditional steed of such hunts, and it proved wise for this one like so many before it.

"So, the miners found this one?" Argus asked, leaning next to the creek and refilling his water skin.

"Aye. They opened up a new cavern of the Deep Mines, but this one led to the surface. They spotted claw marks near the edge of the cave opening along with some scat."

"They haven't seen the creature?" Dorbin asked.

"No. As soon as they saw the signs, they drew back the whole crew. No one wants to anger a garvawk by intruding on its territory."

"No." Dorbin agreed.

"Near an open cave... Sounds te me that we might have a nightcrawler on our hands," Kel reasoned.

"Aye," Lotmeag agreed. "We'll set up in the small valley near the cave and wait for it to come out at night for feeding. Then, we'll be able to put eyes on the creature."

The other garvawk warriors agreed. Felton took everything in, trying to learn all that he could during this hunt. He would be a garvawk warrior, should everything go accordingly, and these were things he thought he should know.

Lotmeag stood up and patted Grub on the side of his big shaggy shoulder. He looped his water skin on the saddle and pulled an apple out of one of the pouches. He held it in front of the great war-hog who gobbled it happily, its wet snout leaving Lotmeag's arm sopping. He shook his head and smiled.

"Did they describe the terrain of the valley to you?" Argus asked quietly, pretending to tighten something on Lotmeag's saddle.

"They did not have much to say about the valley. And I'm not sure I want to capture the beast under open sky, anyway."

"A lot more dangerous," Argus continued the warrior's thought. "You can see them better under open sky, but they are wild and unpredictable. Harder to get them in close."

"Aye," Lotmeag scratched at his chin through his thick brown beard. "And if they have room to dive..."

"Right."

"We'll see what the area looks like. Then we'll make our plan."

Argus didn't say anything. He pressed his lips together in an approving smile and patted Lotmeag on the shoulder. He would lead this *glendon* team just fine. And the old mage had great hope for the younger dwarf's future as a leader of the garvawk warriors.

They loaded back into their saddles. Lotmeag clicked and Grub lurched into motion, leading the group along the creekside and around a bend.

Onward they rode.

While they were still a few miles away from the cave, as marked by the miners, the *glendon* team set up a makeshift corral for the war-hogs. It would do them no good to bring the war-hogs too close to the garvawk's home. The creature's panther-like nose would smell them quickly, and likely find them to be an easy snack while they were penned in. They roped several trees that framed a nice grassy knoll for the war-hogs to enjoy. They put together a pile of fruits and vegetables in the center to keep the hogs focused toward the middle. Most of the time, this sort of pen worked just fine while war-hog riders were out in the mountains on patrol for a few weeks at a time.

The *glendon* team gathered their packs, double-checked their gear and headed off on foot. They still had several miles of mountain terrain to cover before they made it to the valley with the new cave opening that the miners had discovered. Their heavy boots left deep prints in the mud as they walked along the last bit of creek-side trail. They filled their water skins one more time before heading northeast around a mountain bend. They would have to hustle in order to get to the valley in time to scout it prior to nightfall.

They clambered over craggy ridges and passed through narrow valleys filled with trees. If they were lucky, the valley where the garvawk's cave was located would be situated below the tree line and the team would have the added advantage of cover. The more they climbed, however, the more Lotmeag worried that they would not be so lucky.

After another couple of hours, they began to descend along a narrow pathway that had been etched by water runoff. Lotmeag shot a glance over to Argus as they descended back into a treed valley. The old mage nodded. This was fortunate.

They came out on another lower ridge that edged the valley like a ring. Dorbin climbed a small hill to the top of an overlook that gave him a view of the entire valley. He turned to Lotmeag and signaled to the team leader that he could see the cave in question. It was a little lower than their current position and carved straight into the side of the mountain that they had just descended.

The rest of the dwarves joined Dorbin atop the lookout point.

"Alright," Lotmeag started. "The trees in this valley will give us plenty of cover to hide. We'll need to roll in the mud to mask our scent."

"Yeah, especially Dorbin," Kel said.

The dwarves snickered quietly. Lotmeag was glad for their high spirits. A good attitude would help keep them all encouraged if the garvawk proved difficult to capture.

"We'll set up around the cave, hidden among the trees. Owl calls only. Wait until ye see the creature. No calls before then. Hopefully, the garvawk will leave the cave early for dinner."

"Are we trying to get into the cave while the beast is away?" Dorbin asked.

"I think that would be the wisest decision," Argus offered.

"That's the plan. We'll wait 'til the creature's gone and then we'll get into the cave."

"We don't know if it's male or female?" Dorbin inquired.

"No. We'll need to be wary. If there are cubs, we'll have to abort," Lotmeag said with a hint of disappointment at the very real possibility. "But the miners left as soon as they realized they were seeing garvawk sign."

"They wouldn't have explored further," Argus reasoned. "They usually get out of the area quickly and report it."

"Aye," Lotmeag agreed. "Once we find out if there are cubs or not, we'll make the call. Getting between a mother garvawk and her babies is not how I want to die. Any of ye?"

They all shook their heads in response.

"Everyone has their nets?" Lotmeag asked.

"Aye."

"Yeah."

"Yes."

"Good," Lotmeag answered with an approving nod. "We'll get ourselves hidden in the cave as best we can and set our trap. If all goes to plan, we'll catch the beast with our nets, all the netters will hold it down, and Argus will cast the spell to turn it to stone."

"Right," Argus agreed. "I'll mark the garvawk with the rune. Then when I'm done, Felton, you will speak the words to the creature to wake it."

"Yes, sir," Felton replied with a determined tip of his head.

Lotmeag smiled at the war-hog rider. He had known Felton for many years and he couldn't have picked a better dwarf to be joining their ranks. He had a great sense of pride to be the one leading this *glendon* team and bringing Felton into the brotherhood. He smacked a thick dwarven hand onto Felton's shoulder and his jaw clinched into a tight grin. "Let's get to it, then."

The *glendon* team spread out after they found a muddy area in the shade of a thick copse of pines. They had covered themselves and checked each other over to ensure that none would get sniffed out by the garvawk. They each made their way slowly toward the cave and found places to hide among the trees. Lotmeag found a nice fallen tree that rested unevenly, leaving a nice tunnel for the dwarf to hide under and watch the cave.

Night was falling quickly now, and the valley was quiet. The high mountain air was chilly, but the hardy dwarves stayed still under their cover. None of them moved or made a sound.

As the sun finally disappeared behind a nearby western peak, leaving orange and pink streaks of light blazing through the partly clouded sky, they heard a noise.

Hoot! Hoo!

Someone had spotted the garvawk. All of them strained to see the beast at the mouth of the cave. Lotmeag wasn't sure who had signaled the team, but someone had caught sight of the creature. And then they all saw it.

Roooaaarr!

The mighty cry of the garvawk was an awe-inspiring sound. The giant black cat stepped out under the darkening night sky. It stretched its wide bat-like wings and roiled its back, popping several vertebrae and then shaking out its sleep. It padded a few steps forward before flapping its wings and lifting off into the night.

The *glendon* team watched the great cat fly away over a ridge to the north, silently giving thanks that it had not gone over the ridge to the south where their war-hogs had been penned. Still no one moved, all waiting for the signal.

Lotmeag took a deep breath, cupped his hands over his mouth, and let out a loud, *"Hoot! Hoo!"*

It didn't take the team long to reconvene at the entrance to the cave. Lotmeag waved Dorbin and Kel down a passage on the left, while he and Felton searched one to the right. Argus explored a nearby alcove just to make sure they didn't miss anything. After ten minutes of searching, another owl call sounded and echoed off of the stone walls. Dorbin and Kel had found the garvawk's den.

Lotmeag, Felton, and Argus caught up to the two garvawk warriors. "What have ye got?" Lotmeag asked.

"This looks to be the den," Kel answered.

"Good low ceilings. Lots of stalactites," Dorbin added.

"Yes. And plenty of pillars for us to hide behind," Argus offered.

Lotmeag took a second to survey the area and confirm the report. They were right, of course. The three of them had been on plenty of *glendon* teams and he trusted their judgment.

"Alright, then," he spoke to the team in hushed tones. "Argus, ye'll go to the back of the cavern and hide there. If we're lucky, the beast will come back with a fresh kill in its mouth and won't be able to smell us. Then we'll jump out and net him."

"Make sure yer hooks aren't twisted," Dorbin said to Felton.

"Aye," Lotmeag agreed. "Once we've got it netted, Argus will join us and turn the beast to stone."

Each of the dwarves was assigned a pillar or stalagmite to hide behind. They chose them specifically so that they might surround the garvawk.

Lotmeag checked the hooks on the corners of his net. The nets all had hooks on each corner and stone weights on each side. Ideally, the netters would each get their nets over the garvawk. The hooks on each net would catch the other nets and create a tangled mess while the weights helped to shape the net around the beast. Each net also had a woven rope that, when pulled, would tighten the net even more. It sounded rather complicated to those who'd never been on a *glendon* team, but after many years of success, the garvawk warriors had gotten pretty good at the practice. Having four netters usually helped too; because inevitably, one of the nets would not hook. But usually, three was enough for the catch.

Lotmeag leaned around his pillar to look at Felton. He gave the dwarf a proud, excited smile and an approving nod. As long as nothing went wrong, Felton would be part of the garvawk warrior brotherhood by the end of the night.

Several hours went by while they waited in the garvawk den. The night had grown even darker outside, but the dwarves' eyes had adjusted quite well to the dim of the small cavern. The pure adrenaline that pumped through their veins because of anticipation made them hot and caused them to sweat more than they liked.

And then it came.

Rrrrr...

A growl rang out through the tunnels and into the den. It was not a vicious growl but more a satisfied, victorious grumble.

Lotmeag froze. Every muscle in his body tensed.

In walked the garvawk.

The great cat's wings stretched and furled several times as it padded toward the middle of the den. In its mouth, the beast dragged a large portion of some creature that hadn't stood a chance against the predator. *A mountain goat?* Lotmeag guessed. It was just as he had hoped. The garvawk had eaten its fill, hopefully making it slower and restricting its reaction time. But also, the beast had brought back a significant portion of its meal and couldn't smell the hidden dwarfs.

The garvawk dropped the mangled meat on the floor of the den and licked at its claws, trying to clean itself. The great black cat shook its fur and its wings vibrated as it stretched itself out into a relaxed position on the stone floor. The beast seemed quite content with its situation, having had a successful hunt this night.

The dwarves hidden around the chamber stood motionless, poised for their attack.

Lotmeag took in a silent but deep breath.

"*Hoo!*"

It was as if everything in the chamber moved in slow motion. Each of the dwarves jumped out from behind their hiding places, turning to face the garvawk. In only a split second, the great cat jumped into the air, trying to unfurl its bat-like wings. Unfortunately for the garvawk, the surprise had caught it so off guard that it hit several stalactites and fell to the ground again.

The dwarves took the opportunity and launched their nets. Each net hit the garvawk as it writhed and scratched, its wings flapping wildly as it tangled itself deeper in the knotted mess.

"I'll be a bearded gnome!" Kel cursed. His net hadn't caught on with the others.

"Re-throw! Re-throw!" Lotmeag hollered over the garvawk's hissing and roars.

The dwarves pulled their ropes, tightening the nets as Kel did his best to throw his tangled net over the garvawk again.

The beast heaved itself awkwardly and lunged out at Felton, swiping a great gash across the dwarf, ripping into his shoulder between the armor plates.

"Arghh!" Felton cried, dropping his line.

Lotmeag's eyes went wide. Three netters could usually hold a garvawk, but not two. The great cat tried to jump and escape with a renewed ferocity.

"Felton! Grab hold of yer line!" Lotmeag screamed at him.

Felton, having gotten past the initial shock of the garvawk's attack, ran headlong at the beast. He charged straight into the great cat with his good shoulder, toppling it over with another roar. The dwarven warrior rolled away, grabbing his line as he did in a rather acrobatic move.

"Argus!" Lotmeag yelled as Kel also managed to get his tangled net hooked atop the garvawk.

The old mage stepped out from behind a pillar near the back of the den and raised his scepter. Magic had already begun swirling around him before he appeared, ready for his part. He swung the scepter forward, lobbing a ball of mystical energy that slammed into the furious garvawk. The great cat roared even louder. But soon, it stopped fighting. Its roars turned into angry mews like a giant barn cat. It did not know what was happening, but its body was getting harder to move.

Stone crept up the limbs of the garvawk, engulfing its hind quarters and up to the tips of its wings. As the stone slowly enveloped the great cat running up its neck toward its head, the creature let out one more confused cry.

Finally, the garvawk sat as an awkward statue underneath the tangled mess of nets.

"Well done," Argus congratulated the team. "Very well done. She's beautiful."

"Felton," Lotmeag hurried to the dwarf's side, inspecting his bloody armor. "Are ye all right?"

"Just a scratch," he replied with a smile. "I suppose she knew we'd be marking her and thought it fair to mark me, too."

Lotmeag's worry contorted into an amused grin. He patted Felton on the shoulder, who winced.

"Oh! Sorry!" Lotmeag said quickly with a chuckle.

Argus walked up to the stone garvawk as the others cut away the netting and Felton untied the saddle that he had lashed to his back. The old mage waved his fingers over his scepter, mumbling some incantation that the others did not know. Argus's hand began to glow, and he extended his index finger out, writing a runic symbol onto the stone garvawk's shoulder. Kel helped Felton situate the saddle, a rather difficult task with the creature petrified at such an odd angle.

Once everything was ready, Felton took a stance right in front of the garvawk, while the rest of the dwarves resumed their hiding spots. The *glendon* team always did this to ensure that the garvawk's warrior would be the first one it saw.

"You remember the words?" Argus called from his hiding spot, watching Felton stand before the stone creature.

"Yes, sir."

"Then it is yours to say."

Felton took a step forward, inspecting the garvawk for a moment. He pressed his thick dwarven fingers into the crease of his shoulder and rubbed at the blood on his fingers. He chuckled to himself and refocused on the garvawk. He leaned in close and whispered, "*Elocet niol.*"

The stone fell away from the great cat as it stretched its wings and adjusted itself into a standing position on all four of its paws. It looked at Felton with mild confusion, but sat calm before the dwarf. Felton reached his hand up and the garvawk twitched slightly.

"It's alright, now," Felton told her. "Yer with me now, and I'll protect ye."

He brushed the garvawk's panther-like head and scratched around its ear.

The garvawk purred.

The others revealed themselves as Felton mounted up in the saddle. "Well, I guess I'll be seeing ye at home then."

"Aye, we'll see ye there," Lotmeag nodded.

Felton and his garvawk walked to the exit of the cave, the others not far behind, and launched off into the night sky.

Argus patted Lotmeag on the shoulder. "Well done."

"Well done, everyone," Lotmeag replied. "We've got a new brother among the warriors!"

The *glendon* team leader stood on the ledge overlooking the mountain valley bathed in the moonlight. Felton would return home to Galium and the garvawk warriors would celebrate his arrival like they had done with every other warrior that joined their ranks.

Lotmeag, Argus, Dorbin, and Kel would walk the several miles back to the war-hogs. There, Grub and the others would be waiting for them. The dwarves would ride the rest of the night and get home sometime the next day.

Part of him wished that the night would never end. He was overwhelmed with emotion. He had led his first *geldon* team, and they had successfully caught a garvawk and brought a new brother into their ranks. He wasn't sure if there was any greater feeling than the one he experienced now.

This had been a good hunt.

ACKNOWLEDGEMENTS

Thank you for reading my book! I hope you had as much fun getting to know these characters as I did writing the start of their adventure. If so, please leave a wonderful review. Reviews are the lifeblood of indie authors like me. The more positive reviews we have, the more likely it is that others will pick up the book as well.

This book is only a reality because of the flood of encouragement from many readers who have loved these characters. Thank you for that.

Brittany and Crystal, thank you for your dedication and support on these prelude stories. I couldn't have put this collection together without you guys.

ABOUT THE AUTHOR

Z.S. Diamanti is an author, illustrator, and creator. His debut novel, *Stone & Sky,* is an epic fantasy adventure and the result of his great passion for fun and fantastical stories. He went to college forever and has too many pieces of paper on his wall. He is a USAF veteran of Operation Enduring Freedom and worked in ministry for over 10 years. He and his wife reside in Colorado with their four children where they enjoy hikes and tabletop games.

You can explore more of the world of Finlestia and the *Stone & Sky* series at zsdiamanti.com

Connect with him on social media: @zsdiamanti

CONNECT

CONTINUE THE ADVENTURE!

READ THE FIRST BOOK IN
THE STONE & SKY SERIES

ORDER NOW!

Good reviews are vital for Indie Authors. The importance of reviews in helping others find and take a chance on an indie author's book is impossible to overstate.

If you enjoyed this book, would you help me get it in front of more people by taking a minute to give it a good review?
I can't tell you how thankful I'd be.

Check out this link for the best places to review this book and help me get it to more readers who love good books just like you and me!